mothers

of

our

own

little

love

mothers of our own little love

Jesse Eagle

atmosphere press

Published by Atmosphere Press

Cover art by Annette Farrell
Cover design by Kevin Stone

atmospherepress.com

For Mom and Dad.

My sister looked especially criminal that night, like a portrait of a bloodthirsty queen, or some under-wraps vandal, with her cream skin and smoke eyes caught in lamp shadows. It was Sunday night, and every Sunday night we cycled through the same stories about our birth mother. We remembered how our mother would kneel next to our beds and whisper in a strange Italian tongue, or how on certain mornings she'd tape a page of newspaper to the TV screen so we couldn't watch, or how she'd accidentally sliced her arm open in the shower, or how one winter evening she opened the kitchen window and threw dead roses onto the snow below and hyena-laughed as they landed. My sister stopped that particular story to bite her bottom lip until it burned white. "If she came back and saw us like this, almost grown, she'd take us back in a split second," she said. Out in the hallway, one of the other kids was listening. His name was Boom Charlie and he'd been in the home for what seemed like forever. There was even a cigar box full of his baby teeth under his bed. He poked his head into our room, an undone safety pin stuck in the palm of his hand, a drop of blood, and said, "If your mom does come back, she'll come back all different. But she's not coming back."

We were huddled in our room, under a blanket, peeking out through a hole we'd ripped in the wool, watching the hallway. The group home was a deranged factory, all the kids up and alive, wearing new temperatures, animal dancing, like the thunderstorm had finally let them live. One of the younger kids danced past our bedroom door with a flashlight duct-taped to the top of his head, speaking his own language like a tiny new god. Police sirens moved through the city and lightning flashed on the walls and my sister and I pulled the blanket tighter, grinding our teeth, the hairs on our arms standing up, the lightning flashing a few more times before something ancient flooded from the sky and a chorus of thunder cracked so raw and loud and low it seemed to shake all underground. There was a silence, a long silence, and then what sounded like every kid in the home screamed their hearts out in some sick unison. They were urging it on, screaming for the storm to tear everything to pieces, but I remember I wasn't sure if I wanted to destroy the world yet, so I moved closer to my sister under the blanket, and, after a long time, probably somewhere near dawn, the storm finally calmed and we slowly calmed too and closed our eyes to sleep, but it was only temporary.

The group home was an L-shaped building on a corner of Clark Street in Chicago, with eight makeshift bedrooms that fit two kids each, and five much smaller, single rooms if things got crowded, which usually only happened around Christmas. The dining room was the largest room, with an array of tables, mostly donated, some with a polished finish and some with scratches, stains, and burns. Most of the food was donated too, or fundraised, and sometimes a restaurant, like the Italian place down the street or the Ethiopian place a couple blocks south, would send us the works. Sally, the director of the group home, would then send a couple kids to that restaurant, usually the best behaved, and they'd thank them for the contribution and take pictures with the owners for possible publicity. The three bathrooms in the home were all decorated differently, the kids getting their say in certain configurations of frayed towels and toothbrushes, and most of us would use the bathroom nearest our bedroom, the bathroom we'd then have to clean, although some kids, like Boom Charlie, used all three bathrooms so he had to clean all three. There were two main hallways, the L, with one hallway ending at Sally's office, which used to be a stockroom, but had been converted a long time ago, in one of many renovations of the home, and the other hallway ending at Martha, the counselor's, bedroom. The small lobby, where kids first got dropped off, usually by Social Services, had an old blue couch, street rescued, and double glass doors that we kept locked if we weren't going in or out, because, as Martha said, "You never know what'll come walking in off the street."

One kid at the home always thought about his move forever. It was his economic weakness. My sister watched him like a clock, tying and untying her shoe, messing with her neon laces, pretending not to pay attention, even though she was inside his head. He tapped on his queen. "I got nothing solid," he said. He finally moved his knight and as soon as he took his finger off the piece, my sister slid her bishop across the board and slammed it down next to his queen. That was his last day living there. I don't remember his name, but he'd found a foster family, something nuclear, and we thought we'd never see him again, but a few months later he was back at the home with his foster mother, who looked like holographic royalty in a white sundress, gold jewelry, and bleached blond hair. She was meeting with Sally for some reason, probably behavioral, and during their meeting my sister, that kid, and I sat in the hallway right across from his old room and talked about her, his new foster mother, and about his new home, about what it was like. "I mostly stay in my room and check my pulse and write my heartbeat down in a notebook," he said. He then reached in his pocket, a couple bruises on his bicep, and pulled out a river rock, probably from a rock bed at his new house, and rubbed it between the palms of his hands like it was a stick to start a fire. When the rock was warm, he pressed it against his neck and it slipped out of his hand and fell inside his shirt and we all laughed like it might catch the fabric and burn.

About ten of us were outside on the corner, smoking half-frozen sunset cigarettes and watching cars slide around on the ice. One kid was pushing the crosswalk button over and again and each time the stoplight turned red we screeched like something electrocuted and threw rock snowballs at the stopped cars. Martha, who heard our screeching from inside, came stomping out to make sure we weren't smoking, a book under her arm as usual. She was nineteen or twenty and something singular and silk, with a spine like a dog whistle and a short, hard memory. Supposedly her father was a newsworthy killer who was still in prison, one of the older kids telling us how the cops had caught him on the L, basically naked, with streaks of blood across his face and deep cuts in his chest. Most of us didn't believe it though, because Martha was so gentle she couldn't come from vicious blood. Sometimes she'd even allow me in her room to watch her read, her pastel eyes vibrating, her hangnail fingernail moving down the page, and I remember how once I tried to climb in bed with her, but she mercifully kneed me away and called down the hall for my sister and soon Sarah was standing in the doorway, brushing her teeth with her finger, half-awake, her curly hair twisted all over. My sister grabbed my arm and pulled me out of Martha's room and dragged me down the hallway. "Leave her alone. She can't be that for you," Sarah said. But a night or two, when my sister's breathing calmed to a predictable pattern and I knew she was asleep, I snuck down the hallway to Martha's room, where I'd crack open her bedroom door and stand in the doorway and she'd be awake with all her weaponry at the ready.

Chicago was burning music back then. '92 or '93, I can't remember exactly. I was maybe thirteen and Sarah fourteen. We were grinding between skyscrapers, a few minutes late for school, my sister and I holding the metal pole in the center of the train, swaying on the curves, staring out the window, the city waking in split seconds, the apartment buildings like early morning demons in the rising sun. My sister liked to point out the best graffiti, the dying ryes scrawled on the sides of buildings, the hard guns on rooftop ventilation ducts, the yawning fingers somehow painted on the undersides of concrete bridges, the multicolored ridgebacks, the violent algebra, the underground eyes, the slips, the politics. The L burned to a stop and Sarah grabbed my hand and we slid between people and out the door and down the platform. Some of the other kids were walking in front of us, slapping stop signs and talking like bombs, expelling energy before school. "I'm going to show everyone what I'm all about," one of the older girls said. About a block before school there was a kaleidoscope-looking building where my sister and I often stopped, its brick exterior crumbling and the windows smashed by rocks. The faded sign, which was painted on the side of the building, but almost removed by weather, read something about chickens and feed. Even if we were late for school, my sister and I would make time to stop on the side-walk outside that building and look up at the broken top floor windows for as long as we could, waiting for the face of an apparition, some dead factory bookmaker, or some machine crushed industrial worker, or just some overall city ghost to appear and prove to us that the end was never really the end.

I think I wanted to become an American man, so I sat under the sink in the group home bathroom, picking at mildew between the floor tiles, and watched my sister shower. She was a slick furnace, the way she smoked. The mirrors were all steamed up. I watched her wash her legs with a bar of cracked yellow soap, her toes pointing out, her wet and tangled hair hanging midway down her back, the bruise on the bone of her hip. I remembered how our birth mother used to let us watch TV at night, to calm us down before bed, and how I really wanted to be what I saw on the screen, and how, at the time, I thought what I wanted wasn't too much to want. I just wanted to close my eyes after a long day's work, my wallet on the dresser, my wife, with her beautiful hair, her continental ideas, asleep next to me, in a suburban house with three bedrooms, a fence around the yard, my son and daughter down the hall, both with their own room, both with their own TV, both of them safe. I wanted to never need luck again. I wanted to go to work and look out my office window at the buses and cabs like grease on the street below, adjust my tie, and tell the person on the other end of the phone not to worry, it's going to be alright, you just have to dream, dream, dream, dream, dream, dream, dream motherfucker, this is America, dream and you'll get what you want in the end.

My sister and I were looking down into an open manhole and what wafted up smelled like wilted feet and crusted mustard. Sarah said she saw an animal skull floating in the sewer water, but then she said it was just a workman's boot. Flurries began to fall and a cold wind carved through the city so we buttoned our coats to our chins and walked along Lake Street until we found a building without a doorman. The couches in the lobby were red leather and we snuck across to the elevator and my sister pressed the up button over and over, making a song out of the clicks, a Celine or Mariah. When the doors finally opened, the elevator was empty and the walls were mirrors and the music was a feather piano. We rode to the top floor, the penthouse, while we checked our reflections from all angles, my sister looking closely at her teeth, her incisor topography. She ripped a hang loose piece of skin from her chapped bottom lip, and the elevator opened to a hollow and unfinished floor, with piles of wood, saws, blue tarps, spooled wires, and other machines scattered around. Someone was building something, a durable investment. We went to one of the large windows and from up there everything, even the marquees, even the polished cars, even the people dressed well for work looked dead and battered in the stinging cold.

The girl was wearing a leather jacket, jeans, and black boots and the guy was wearing the same. "She walks like a finger on skin. I need to learn that," my sister said. We left our place on the curb and followed them a few blocks, the guy lighting a cigarette and blowing smoke out the side of his mouth, away from the girl. "He's a bull clown, but I feel like enough assholes will vote for him," we thought we heard the girl say. The rush hour traffic was thick down Ashland, the sun setting just above the buildings, elongating the shadows on the street, the whole scene feeling artificial like we were being filmed, and there we were, in a thriller, stalking this young couple, following them from a safe, predatory distance, my sister kicking an empty shopping cart on the sidewalk a couple times to see what they'd do, shaking the metal loud, but the couple was oblivious and didn't look back. "If he does win, we'll just have to fight everything tooth and nail," the guy said. My sister cracked a couple of her knuckles, and in those cinematic shadows, her fingers looked twice as long as normal, almost like skinny claws. The couple stopped on a busy corner and waited for the walk signal, the girl tugging at the guy's jacket until he bent down and kissed her with an open mouth. I couldn't help but watch my sister as she watched them. There was a strange feather density to her face, a travel to her eyes, her lips moving slowly as though she'd jumped bodies and was now living inside both the girl and guy simultaneously, like she was both sides of that kiss.

The fence behind our birth mother's apartment building was decorated with about a hundred small, red ribbons tied to the chain-link. My sister told me how our mother used to sit cross-legged in the grass in front of that fence and untie each red ribbon every morning, and how, as she untied them, she'd place the ribbons in an urn, an urn that once contained the ashes of our grandmother, but which was now empty. Sarah said that after all the ribbons were untied and placed in our grandmother's urn our mother would come back up to the apartment and set the urn in the very center of the kitchen table, like it was the eye of a star, and then she would carefully, very carefully open it and count the ribbons. "After that, for the rest of the morning, she'd usually sit around the apartment with the empty urn. She had these certain places she'd sit," my sister said. "Like she'd sit on the windowsill at the front window and speak broken Italian to the birds and chain smoke, or she'd sit on top of the kitchen counter, in a dingy, white nightgown, and swat at imaginary flies, or she'd sit cross-legged on the floor in front of the TV, very quiet and still, and just watch static, almost like she was just a body with nothing inside." On summer Saturdays, Sarah told me, before I was born, they'd usually go to the public pool in the neighborhood, where our mother would lie out on a pool chair, chew cinnamon gum, and get some sun. My sister remembered men, and one man in particular, a man who once brought our mother two rabbits in a cage and left the cage next to her chair at the pool. Our mother didn't acknowledged the man, didn't give him the time of day, and he retreated without saying a word, leaving the cage of rabbits to who knows what fate, because our mother didn't take it home, and that night, like every night, at sunset, she was back outside, sitting cross-legged in front of that fence with the urn, retying all the red ribbons.

Sarah woke in a gasp and told me about the dream she'd just had. I'd almost had the same dream. The sewer pipes were made of fused bone and the water inside was a strange molasses and it oozed through the bone pipes in a heavy, slow glob until it reached every faucet in the city. If you drank the water, a thick goop would sit in your stomach until it hardened, and then you'd have to cut open your belly, slide out a single, fist-sized piece of dried molasses stone, this black onyx, and sew yourself up again before you bled to death. My sister and I blossomed awake in our beds, dissecting our dream, a morning light coming through the small window above us, soft and blue, a couple kids arguing out in the hallway. "You can't walk on water, dummy. I don't care what you say," one of the older kids said. I knew his voice. He was the kid who ate dandelions. "I'll prove it. We'll go down to the lake and I'll be walking all over that water," a younger kid said. With the quiet broken, Sarah moaned upright, got her clothes together from a pile on the floor, and went to the bathroom, but I stayed in bed, touching the bone at the top of my spine, where a bug bite had bubbled up overnight. I remember I was thankful that morning, but I'm not sure why. Maybe I was thankful for that home, or maybe for my sister, thankful that I didn't have to dream alone, or maybe it was the bug bite, maybe I was thankful that it gave me something new to touch.

My sister was brushing her teeth with her finger, our toothbrush all crusted again, and spitting the toothpaste in the sink. Her gums never bled and, unlike mine, her teeth were straight. We left the bathroom light on for the next kid and went down to the dining room, where we sat at a table with two other girls and ate breakfast. One of the girls only ate applesauce. She wore clear nail polish and had a birthmark shaped like a pirate key on her neck. She was new at the home. She told us she'd been living in a sinkhole for three days before anyone good found her, told us that everything about her hurt. "I got to feed some gypsy raccoons though. They can remember stuff for three years, like how to open a certain type of soup can," she said. The other girl at the table folded up entire pancakes and shoved them in her wide-open mouth like a drunken dentist. Her name was Sammy, and she had a Walkman with fat foam headphones, and sometimes she'd let me listen to her music so she could study my facial expressions as I did. "That song made you look like a burned-up wolf," she'd say. Or, "That one made you look like an ugly newborn." Or, "I could tell you weren't even trying to hear that one." I told her I liked any song with a piano so she'd rewind those for me, over and over, until she saw something she couldn't describe.

We used to imagine there were cameras in every room of the home, as small as insects, hidden inside precise holes drilled into the ceilings, their hairline cables tangled behind the drywall and strung under the floorboards, running signals down to a secret room in the basement, where a policeman sat at a desk, sipped coffee, and watched us on black-and-white TV monitors. The mayor of the city, Mr. Daley, would sometimes be down there too, with the policeman, watching us. "It's like they want to live inside us. Like it's vicarious," my sister said. She stood on the bed and moved her hand very slowly along the ceiling to search for any newly drilled holes where a camera could be. The sun was setting outside and our bedroom was cold plum and soon Martha busted in to search around before bedtime, opening the top drawer of our dresser and running her hand under our underwear. "This door stays open evenings. I'm not reminding you again," she said and went to the next room. My sister asked for her pajama bottoms, so I opened the top drawer of the dresser, bunched them into a ball, and threw them at her. She checked the pockets to make sure nothing she'd hidden was missing and then looked under her bed, inside a shoebox, for something. For the rest of the night, we played a dozen games of chess, my sister always winning like old money, and when we were finished, she packed up the board, clicked off the bedside lamp, and I remember it took me forever to fall asleep because I kept hearing a camera above me, its lens buzzing, zooming in and out.

Martha had to have a talk with my sister in our bedroom. It was summer and the home was a humid nest, with a bunch of old box fans scattered around, plugged into nearly every socket, the air-conditioning broken again, but the fans barely worked, so a ripe, deep-pit, bacterial smell still rose from the carpets. Most the kids were hanging outside, wandering alleys or riding the L around, trying to find hotel lobby air-conditioning, on the lookout for water, food, and, of course, money. But I was sitting in the hallway on the sour carpet listening to Martha's voice vibrate through the bedroom door in low, desperate tones. It sounded like tornado type of talk, with stuff being thrown around. I was cleaning my shoes with spit when Sammy came in from outside, her headphones on, as usual, her shirt soaked through with sweat and her knee skinned up and bleeding. She saw me in the hallway and sat next to me and I nodded towards the bedroom door. "I heard she's in trouble for taking another car ride," Sammy said, crossing her legs, the blood from her skinned knee dripping down her shin. She gave me the headphones and I listened to a couple songs, a turnkey country ballad and a deep-water symphony, and soon the door swung open and Martha walked out, eyeing Sammy and me. Inside the bedroom my sister was tangled on the bed with her hair hiding her eyes, and "Hey, James, James, James, you like the way that one song sounds so lonely? Like it's the last living cell," Sammy said to distract me.

My sister unstuck her cheek from my shoulder and whispered like she often did when she first woke. "My arms and legs are numb. Sleep demons," she said. It had been another long, scorching summer night. We'd been sleeping under the streetlights on and off for about a week because we could actually breathe outside. Sarah found her lighter, lit a cigarette, put her head back on my shoulder, and smoked. "Do you think we'll remember any of this?" she said. Next to us a few of the group home kids were still sleeping on the grass near the front steps of a church, their shirts pulled over their heads to block the sun and noise. If the cops rolled through, creeping along like they sometimes did, they'd usually let us sleep out there by the church, unless one of the local businesses complained – the accountant, the basement bar down the street, or, most likely, the lawyer who had his office on the corner. My sister smoked three cigarettes in a row and I do remember some of it, Sarah. I remember later that day we walked to an air-conditioned diner, where we ate onion rings and tore napkins into small squares and you said something about how we badly needed a benefactor.

We hid behind parked cars and watched her window. Sometimes she wouldn't be home for what seemed like months and the curtains would be closed and her apartment would be dark, but sometimes we'd walk by and see a light on, and Sarah and I would panic and hide like varmints to try and catch a glimpse of her. One night while we were checking for unlocked car doors, the light in her apartment came on and when we looked up, she was standing right there at her window, so serene, so lily, like a scarved flower. We always imagined she was a biologist – someone who worked with germs in a lab, who risked her life to save ours. My sister and I kept to the shadows and scurried down the sidewalk until we found the perfect hiding spot behind a laundry truck. "God, I hope she's alone," my sister said. We peeked around the bumper of the truck and she was still up there, wearing what looked like a cotton robe, staring directly at where we were hiding. "She looks childless," Sarah said, and we came out from behind the truck and stood in the middle of the street and looked up at her. My sister lit a cigarette, took a couple puffs, and then handed it to me. The light from her window was soft blue electronics and we couldn't hear or see or taste a thing else beyond her fantasy.

My sister searched high and low for her missing $10, blaming Martha, while she told me a story about our mother, about how she used to get letters from all over the world. The letters were from people our mother had met when she was younger, people from Vegas and Detroit and St. Louis and Baltimore, and inside the letters were seashells, mostly the pastel and fragile kind, the kind that are easily broken underfoot. Each time our mother got one of these letters, which was every couple months or so, she'd go make herself a drink and sit by the window. She'd tear the envelope open, shake out the sand, slip the seashells into the palm of her hand, and examine them closely in the sunlight, like the shells were some kind of quiet hope. Sometimes she'd even smell and lick them, and after she was done examining them, she'd place them on the bookcase, next to all the other shells. My sister said there must've been two hundred shells on that bookcase, and when our mother left the apartment to go to the corner store, or the unemployment office, or was sent to the hospital, my sister would lift me up by the waist so I could see them. "You wanted to touch them, but I never let you. I was even afraid they'd break," my sister said as she tossed her dresser drawer for the missing $10. It was another Sunday night and the home was dead quiet because one of the kids, a kid about our age who was ashamed of his stutter, even though it wasn't that bad, had gone to the park three blocks away, climbed the tallest tree, fallen or jumped off, and broken a few bones. He was in urgent care and all of us were quietly hoping, like our mother used to, for his sake, that the fall had somehow reset him.

Boom Charlie was sprawled out on the blue street rescued couch in the lobby, talking to one of the missionaries that came around from time to time. If Sally or Martha ever caught them inside the home, they'd run them off, but today, with Sally at a director's meeting and Martha taking a nap, Boom Charlie got to humor the guy. "I've done a lot of thinking about that, you know. Late-night thinking. About that whole thing, death and heaven. It'll either be pure darkness, the end of all your thoughts, the end of everything really, or, even colder, it'll be what you always wanted it to be, your wildest dreams. Like a basketball court floating in space, or a penthouse full of steak. But I really don't think there's a heaven or hell. There isn't anything," Boom Charlie said. The missionary folded and refolded a corner of a pamphlet he'd brought, the literature. He kept trying to interrupt Boom Charlie as the kid explained the logistics of his basketball court in space, the spinning stars like rabid fans, the polished hardwood, the smell of it like the smell of his mother before the drugs, lavender citrus, the piped-in music, which played dope classics after every dunk, and when the missionary finally flat-out interrupted Boom Charlie by speaking over him, Boom Charlie simply got up and walked out, past my sister and I as we listened from the hallway. The missionary stayed on the couch for a long time after, picking the lint off his white dress shirt, maybe waiting for another kid to wander into the lobby, but we knew better, so finally he rolled up his shirtsleeves and hit the bricks.

There were these kids, these kids who lived in a city, a cold city where the streets were crowded, where people screamed their lungs out on the corners, where stray dogs ate trash from the gutters, where skyscrapers were built so close together they rubbed against one another, rubbed because of the wind or because of the shifting and sinking streets, and sometimes this rubbing made sparks, sparks the size of human heads, sparks that fell onto the sidewalks, fell onto the people, onto the full-grown, the adults, but these adults, these full-grown, they kept walking the streets like the sparks were nothing, dodging them if they could, going to work, and always, always wearing their masks. Some of the full-grown wore the masks of birds, of eagles and ospreys, and some wore the masks of sea creatures, of sharks and stingrays. The kids hated these masks, so they'd sneak around, hiding inside elevators or in alleyways or in streetlight shadows, and they'd watch the full-grown closely, studying how they moved, how they ate, and how they spoke. And one lonely night, on this one particular night, the kids decided to gather on the rooftop of the tallest skyscraper in the city, and up there the wind was a scar and the stars were missing from the sky and the traffic below was a snake, and these kids began to rock back and forth on that rooftop, back and forth, shoulder to shoulder, hundreds or thousands of millions of kids, and the skyscraper began to twist and bend and rub against its neighboring skyscraper, and sparks began to fall, and the sparks these kids caused were gigantic, much larger than any spark before, much larger than any human head, and these gigantic sparks rained down onto the street, rained down onto the full-grown in their masks as they went to work, and the kids kept twisting and bending and rubbing the skyscraper, the sparks becoming larger and larger, until finally, the whole city burned.

Sarah's blankets were bunched at the bottom of her empty bed and her pillow was on the floor. I stayed in bed for a few more minutes, in limbo, thinking about the dream I'd just had, cycling through watery, snapshot images from what I thought was a beautiful, burning future while I looked at the chipped paint on the ceiling, searching for cameras. It was going to be a deep boil of a day. In the little mirror on the dresser, I checked my teeth and eyes, both decaying in strange directions, and then went out to the dining room, where Sarah was sitting with an older girl, a girl who'd once asked a couple of us to show her our everything in an alley. I told Sarah about the dream I'd just had, about how the skyscrapers were swaying and sparking, how the streets were blind butchers, how there was an injured dog in a gutter with a deep, dark hole in her stomach from a bullet wound, how we could burn it all down together. My sister said she hadn't dreamt at all last night and the other girl said nobody wanted to hear about other people's dreams. It was a claw to the jaw, so I grabbed the last box of the best tooth-rot cereal, and sat by myself at another table, but I wasn't as hungry anymore.

Boom Charlie tried to sneak into the home first thing in the morning, all broken up. He was holding his right arm like a cradled baby and his face was bloodied, his eye nearly swollen shut and his bottom lip split down the middle. A few of us helped him to his room and into his bed, gently pulling his shirt over his head and draping a blanket across his legs. His back and chest were bruised, with purple inkblots on his dark skin, and when one of the kids asked him what'd happened he pushed down on a squid-shaped bruise on his shoulder and said, "I shouldn't have been messing around with those guys." And because there was no hiding this from her, my sister went to get Martha while the rest of us stood around Boom Charlie. After a few minutes, his eyes closed and he looked like he'd entered a tussle dream, his body twitching into the fetal position, his right arm, at the femur, swelling like he had a bad break. He coughed a couple times, cracked open his swollen eye, and gave a snicker, his lip still bleeding. "All I did was ask one of them if they knew my cousin. That's what you get for asking questions," he said, turning to his side so he could rest on his good arm. "You got to be worried about everybody. I really wish it wasn't that way, but that's the way," he said.

My sister smashed a square of margarine into the middle of her mashed potatoes and watched it melt. She did the same thing on my plate. "I love the way solids become liquids," she said. Across the dining room, at a table in the corner, Martha sat by herself, staring at a plastic peach cup, a book face down in front of her. She looked god heavy, with dark circles under her eyes and greasy hair, like she'd been in her memory all night, like she'd been dragged around in the past. My sister kicked me under the table and mouthed what I already knew, so I walked over to Martha's table and stood quietly next to her. "Not now, James. Please," she said. Up close, her face was a cavity, like maybe she was becoming her father, like she could kill if she wanted to. She opened her book and pretended to read, but I knew it was all a facade. She even pretended to run her finger down the page and mouth the words. "Please leave, James. Jesus," she said, so I walked away to get a square of margarine and a plate of mashed potatoes. I unwrapped the square and smashed it in the middle of the potatoes and brought the plate over to Martha. I didn't know how else to help her.

Things in the home felt like they were evaporating. Martha had been missing for a couple weeks, leaving all her stuff behind, even her books, all of us kids thinking the worst, missing her, but then one afternoon, out of the living blue, she showed up with her head shaved. We kept asking her where she'd been and, to shut us up, she said, "I met someone new, but she didn't turn out to be who she said she was." After that, I realized anybody could leave at any time, so I started hiding under my sister's bed while she slept to keep an eye on her. The bottom of her mattress would expand and contract with her breathing and often she'd talk in her sleep – a wild, vanishing type of talk, like she was running from all things hideous. And I remember one night while I was under there and dead tired, or half-dead, or something, I heard Sarah get up at three in the morning, toss her blanket to the floor, and dissolve down the hallway. What felt like a long time later, she came back, whispering, repeating something like, "I need to go home. Let's just go home. Let's go home. It's time to just go home," and climbed back into bed. I listened to her whisper her new mantra until she fell asleep again, and I must've fallen asleep too, because in the morning I woke to what sounded like the new kid crying somewhere in the home. He'd lost the Saint Barbara necklace his mother had given him and was accusing everybody of taking it. I yawned and rolled over and my sister was right there next to me, under the bed, staring craters into my face with her black olive morning eyes, and we stayed like that, face to face, still and staring, until the fireworks with the necklace hit the finale.

Some kid at the home pulled a gun from his jacket pocket and tossed it on his bed. It was wrapped in a frayed bandana. He said he could kill anyone now, that he finally had some power. "My brother gave it to me to hide, so best not tell anyone," he said. The next morning when I was in the dining room, watching Martha eat her peach cup, I wanted to tell her about the gun, but I didn't know what the kid was capable of, didn't know the exact score, so I let it soak. I finished breakfast and went to the bathroom and when I came back to our room my sister wasn't there, so I searched around the home until I finally found her. She was sitting next to the kid on his bed, with the gun in her lap, holding it like a baby. "It's heavy," she said. "Feels bigger than it is." After that Sarah started dragging me downtown with the kid, where we'd mostly sit on the bench in front of a famous fire station, smoke cigarettes, and stare at the hospital across the street. "They keep all the sick kids on the top floor. Probably so they can get a better view before they die," the kid said. He was smoking a cigarillo, the frayed bandana from the gun tied around his head. A cop car pulled up to the stoplight and the cop inside looked over at us, his sunglasses tinted silver. "I could shoot him, you know," he said. "But I'm not dumb. There's too many of them and we'd eventually lose."

Sally, the director of the group home, had lost her daughter, Abigail, to a rare disease years before and one night, after a small girl had been adopted earlier in the day, the girl saying her shy goodbyes with her favorite pink pillow clutched to her chest, Sally decided to tell a few Abigail stories. About a half dozen kids were gathered in the dining room, resting on each other, eating Italian ices, feeling sorry for ourselves, when Sally, who could be private as a church, came in and sat with us. She took off her old army jacket, her arms skinny and her wrists all bone, and told us about how Abigail used to lie about the strangest things, like saying there was a crashed seaplane buried in their backyard, or that she was a witchdoctor and knew how to bring back the gods, or that she, and only she, knew the deepest kind of math, that she knew the numbers that could cure anything. And once, Sally said, as she messed with the charm bracelet on her wrist, on the front steps of their building, Abigail fell and knocked out one of her baby teeth, but she didn't come crying to Sally. Instead, she searched for her tooth for over an hour, finally finding it by combing the grass, and then calmly examined it like it was more than bone. Sally stopped her story, put her army jacket back on, told us the next family would be our family, and hugged a little kid who was sitting backwards on his chair, a boy who was afraid to take off his shoes.

One of the girls had said something about Sarah's ear again, something like, "You'd be so pretty if it wasn't folded over like that," and my sister sat there, her smirk a vulture's. I knew the mayhem that followed, so I grabbed her hand under the dining room table, squeezed her fingers, and whispered, "Don't, Sarah," but then another girl decided to say something else, something about the guy who sometimes came by to pick Sarah up in his car, something like, "That dude looks like a movie monster. He's got orb eyes," and my sister ripped her hand away from mine, grabbed her fork and knife, jumped up on the table, kicked both girls' food to the floor, and began pacing back and forth on the tabletop like death on a deathbed. It was only a butter knife, but she had this look in her eyes like she would maim us all. I looked around the dining room for Martha to come calm the situation, but she wasn't there, a kid running down the hallway to get her. My sister saw the scene she was causing, stopped stomping around in my mashed potatoes, jumped off the table, and sat next to me like nothing had happened, the two girls not daring move an inch, afraid to even itch, frozen there as captured prey.

The final time my sister and I were left alone in that apartment I remember as red, white, and blue. Red because Sarah cut off the tip of her finger trying to make us dinner, white because her face went pale before she passed out, and blue because our mother always told us never to call the cops, under any circumstances, never call the figlio un cane cops, but my sister was on the floor with the tip of her finger clutched in her hand and a bucket of blood on her shirt, and I was young, probably seven or eight, and panicked, leaning over her, shaking her shoulders and yelling her name. She regained consciousness for a minute and whispered something inaudible, but then her already distant eyes rolled to the back of her head and she passed out again. The severed part of her finger was mostly fingernail, with some white bone inside, a ripped thread of dangling skin, so I broke down and called 911 and soon two paramedics stomped into our apartment carrying bags of equipment. They hovered over her, shaking her awake to ask her simple questions that she could barely answer, attempting to get to the bottom of the situation. They finally bandaged her hand and brought her downstairs on a stretcher and I rode up front with the ambulance driver to the hospital, my eyes pickled, the siren blaring down Ashland, the city blurred to simple shapes, to basic architecture. The doctor at the hospital said I did well by calling 911 and gave me a strong clap on the back like a father would. He also asked about our mother, how long she'd be away, how long we'd been alone, and I hadn't perfected my lies yet.

We wandered around Uptown checking car doors until we finally found an unlocked sedan on some side street, the car rusted to the heart, the metal of the wheel wells eaten away like clown teeth, the windshield cracked to a spider web. My sister climbed inside anyway, looking for money, opening the glove box and searching the ashtray, pulling down the sun visors, but of course there was no change. Under the passenger seat, she found some waterlogged envelopes bound together by rubber bands, so she grabbed them, and we ran to an alley, where we sat on a loading pallet and opened the first letter. My sister said it was a doctor's bill for thousands. She said the man to whom the letter was addressed had been blind for years, with a worm inside his brain. She wouldn't let me see the letter, but she read, "Sir, I'm sorry this condition is unfortunately terminal, yet I still must insist you pay your bill. Signed, Dr. Mads Love." I didn't believe her, didn't believe her bourgeoisie diction, didn't believe the Dr.'s name, so Sarah opened the next letter, which she said was from the man's wife. "Dearest, Louis, I am a heartache now. That worm, that terrible creature that found its way into your ear as you slept drunk in the park, has burrowed into our lives and taken everything from us, from our child. Do you remember that morning, that morning after the worm had crawled inside your brain and you woke completely blind, and you, after realizing this, cried out, cried out like a madman, cried out for me, your sweet wife? Oh, Louis, such panic, such despair, as you felt blindly around our apartment, felt around for your shoes, for your clothes, for the kitchen knives, which I'd already hid, hid so you wouldn't cut open your arms like mother did. Do you remember how you blindly felt your way to the front door, like braille felt your way down the hallway, to the elevator, to the lobby, to the street, where someone immediately kicked you straight in the ribs, some business-man, those businessmen, even worse than the worm itself. Oh Dearest, do you remember how you felt your way along the sidewalk, along the gutters, to the tavern, and how you could hear everything so clearly once you started drinking again. You could hear a phone ring a hundred blocks away, in some dusty old apartment, you could hear the ocean waves on the other side of the world, you could hear life and death come and go. How you loved hearing the whole world like that, Louie, loved it more than seeing a hundred miles straight and true to your dear wife and beautiful young son waiting for you, here."

Supposedly, in the '70s, the group home was a funeral home, which was probably why the basement smelled like swollen skin. Martha stood at the top of the stairs, searching for the string to the light bulb, tipping to her toes, trying not to fall downstairs. She finally found the string and the bulb crackled on and our eyes adjusted to the yellowed dark. There was an abandoned casket with its header open in the corner, below a small, caked, street-level window, and, at the far end of the basement, two more caskets were upright against the wall, both closed, one of them with a winding crack across its cherry wood. "A crisp nests for spiders," Martha said as we rummaged around downstairs, rearranging rusted, leftover folding chairs, a pissed mattress or two, and a bunch of unmarked boxes until she found the backup vacuum and its plastic tube extensions. The vacuum was heavy and the wheels had broken off, so she dragged it to the bottom of the stairs and yelled up for one of the older kids to come down and help, but no one answered. I told her I could help her carry it and we slowly made our way upstairs, my arms burning and my hands slipping until I finally got a good grip about halfway up. "I never want to be in a casket underground. If you're still around, cremate me," Martha said. We took a breath at the top of the stairs and dusted off our hands, Martha reaching up to click off the light, and for a moment you could hear all the kids stomping around above.

A woman was pushing a shopping cart down the street, hunched over, her hair wild and white. In the cart, there were stacks of books wrapped with twine, some street aluminum, burnt plastic bottles, and spools of string. Her shoes looked brand new, but her purple t-shirt was faded to something like tie-dye. She stopped on the corner to cough into a paper napkin she pulled from her pocket, the heavy traffic heaving exhaust, so hot that day the street seemed a mirage. She coughed and coughed, coughing so hard she had to drop to a knee right there on the sidewalk and grab hold of the shopping cart for support. "She's in a bad way," my sister said. The woman's coughing fit continued, and she looked at the sky between hacks, shielding her eyes from the sun, and above the lone cloud split into two smaller clouds and an airplane cut through the huge blue. The sun dug deeper into the street and the woman slowly rose to her feet, put the napkin back in her pocket, pushed her cart up on the curb, and came towards us at the bus stop. As she got closer we could see that her left eye was dead, gray and filmy, with only a faded lilac of a pupil. We helped her pull her cart up to the bus stop and she sat next to us on the bench, my sister asking her which book was her favorite. "The one about winter," she said and the three of us waited for the bus while the world dragged along like loose skin.

An ambulance came blazing up behind us and flew through the intersection without slowing, splashing the sidewalk with gutter water. The rain fell harder and people on the street scattered and hid under awnings and bus stop overhangs. My sister got her cigarettes and lighter from her backpack and we ducked into an alley behind an office building, where she cupped her hands and lit one. We ended up walking the streets all day in the rain, my sister saying it was purifying, and when we finally made it back to the home, she still didn't want to go inside, so we sat on two discarded barstools in an alley and watched the windows of a neighboring apartment building. I knew she was avoiding something, probably the guy who sometimes picked her up in his car, the movie monster, but I didn't say a thing. I just dried my wet hair with the hood of my sweatshirt and listened to some of the kids from the home messing around outside in the rain, their voices echoing from somewhere a few blocks south. "Listen to them. We're just a bunch of street kids roaming around. We'll be out here until there's nothing left," my sister said. She lit her last cigarette, crumpling the pack and throwing it over her shoulder into the dumpster, smoked half of it, and then handed me the rest. A light came on in a third-story window and inside an older man walked around his apartment. He wasn't wearing a shirt and his shoulders were hospital-white and he looked to be moving a picture frame around, from one shelf to another. The sunlight was almost gone and the streetlights were reflecting the raindrops on his window and we stayed in the alley for another half hour and watched the man stare at the picture for way too long.

I've always liked the screeching sound of something going backwards, something rewinding. I gave the Walkman back to Sammy and she slipped the headphones around her neck. "That one song has highway drums," she said. Her eyes were so blue, almost unnaturally, and when she shot me eye contact, which she didn't often do, I'd dizzy up and confuse. When the tape was rewound, she scooted closer to me on her bed and we each shared an ear of headphone and listened to the song with the drums again. I closed my eyes and without thinking I kissed Sammy and that was my first kiss, and she closed her eyes and kissed me back. We sat on the edge of her bed and listened to music together and kissed quickly a few more times and then went quiet. On the nightstand there was a picture of a woman holding a child. The woman was sitting on the hood of a rusted pickup truck, and in the background, behind her, was flat farmland stretching to the horizon, with spiraled bales of hay scattered across a field. I thought the child might be Sammy, but it had brown eyes. Sammy pressed pause on her Walkman and took off the headphones. "That's a picture of my little brother, Ricky," she said. "He died, but it's okay."

We ran down Ashland to catch up with Chuy and his burrito cart. He liked to tell us about how he'd been feeding the kids from the home for ten years, and how he still saw a couple of them, all grown up and doing well, around the neighborhood. He said one of them was a guard down at the prison, and the other one worked insurance over in Rogers Park. "She's always got nice clothes on. Never looks sour," he said. Like always, he gave us a free taco because we bought four, and with the money we'd pooled together Sammy paid for the tacos and an orange soda to share and we sat on a curb across from a Buddhist temple to eat. "I bet you can't name all the presidents in order," Sammy said. The Buddhist temple was an old house repainted pastel blue, with wooden shutters on the windows and a large, rusted bell somehow attached to the roof. In the front yard there was a bronze statue of Buddha and Sammy, after staring at the Buddha for a long time, said she wanted the statue to move, to break free from its cast and walk around, to wink at us, to cry a doomed tear, to surprise us with a miracle, but the statue remained still. We finished the tacos and our soda and held hands as we walked back to the group home, both of us feeling the thermals, maybe even some love, but we were scared about what usually happened next and goddamn that fear was nirvana.

One kid was turning eleven, so we had a party for him. He wouldn't wear his birthday hat or let us sing happy birthday, but he blew out his candles like a madman, spitting all over the cake. Someone asked him what he'd wished for. "Cash and a girl," he said. Someone else said he'd just ruined his wish. "That's just mojo," he told them. He sliced up his birthday cake into some kind of chaos and started handing out misshapen pieces, talking as fast as he could, like an auctioneer. "Who wants a deformed piece? One deformed piece. Still good. Still real good. Tastes the same. Tastes like heaven. Sold, to the kid in the dirty shirt." The kids gathered around him like a mob, so I rushed my way to the front, got a slice of cake shaped like a dead starfish, and handed it to Sammy. One of the younger girls, a newer girl, didn't get a piece, so she began sneaking around to all the tables, trying to swipe at least a finger lick of frosting. An older kid saw what she was doing and pushed her two-handed backwards and she tumbled to the floor, where she stayed, curled up. Like most of us, Sammy had seen it before, so she cut a sliver off our piece of cake and, balancing it on her fork, walked across the dining room to the girl, and the minute the girl saw Sammy coming she bounced up from the floor and stuck out her tongue with ambition.

You could hear it through the walls, the thump of his speakers as he pulled up to the home. The minute my sister heard that bass she hurried to make her bed, her hair still wet from a shower, twisted in anonymous ways, and then rushed outside and jumped in his car. From the window, I watched them pull away, the bass drifting off, the Acura like a smooth top spinning down the street, the windows tinted and the license plate framed by flashing blue lights. Maybe they were going to an apartment with polished hardwood floors and an elevated view of the city, or maybe they were going shopping downtown, to the five-story Nike store, where he might buy her new shoes or even an entire outfit. I made sure the front door of the home was locked, so she'd have to knock to get back inside, a soft rebellion, and then I went to the dining room, but breakfast was already over, with only a couple kids still in there playing bloody knuckles, winging quarters at each other from across the table. Hungry, I wandered around the home, counting whatever chickens I had left, until I saw an older girl's bedroom door open. Her room was perfectly arranged, with dolls posed on her nightstand. "Gunshots or fireworks last night?" she said. She bent down to tie her laces and after she'd double knotted them she said she was bored and asked me if I wanted to go somewhere and just chill, watch stuff, and maybe touch.

She told me she didn't know where she got the cuts on her hands, but she was lying. She'd been climbing barbed wire fences again. "I'm too tired today, James. You always look too close and listen too hard. Let it go," my sister said. We were on our way to Sally's office, stopping to look at the wall, which had something like a cave drawing splattered across the wallpaper, a turtle without a shell, with its spine exposed. "That vandalism is courtesy of Marie. Hurry up, hustle," Sally yelled from her office, so we rushed down the hallway. She told us to shut the door and have a seat, a soft sunlight coming through the window directly behind where she sat at her desk. There were framed pictures of kids everywhere in the room, on the walls and bookcases and coffee table. Some of the kids I knew, like Boom Charlie, Martha, when she was much younger, and Sal, but some I didn't. The largest picture, which was on Sally's desk, was of a girl with freckled skin and braided hair sitting on a park swing. There were two dates, birth and death, etched into the gold frame. "It's no small miracle, but we've found a foster for both of you, together," Sally said. A symphony of nerves and my hands went plumb numb and Sarah catapulted inside her body, which came out as a small shiver. Sally tilted her face toward the sunlight and I remember I was hoping she was thinking about Abigail right then, about how her daughter's lies were never lies at all.

The kids would be studying us closely, after a long meeting with Sally, so we tried our best not to show our luck. We left her office, walked back down the hallway, past Marie's spinal turtle, and straight out the front door, where outside the sun split the street into strange colors, into steel whites and concrete blues. I think I wanted the world to stop right there, for all time to seize, for infinite space to be sucked back into something singular. Sarah was staring at the sky, her eyes stirring, and I could tell she was imagining something, probably our new family, our new home, so I imagined along with her; the bedsheets smelled like detergent roses, and there were small blue triangles on the wallpaper, and the kitchen was modern, with a sleek faucet we could wrap our mouths around and drink, the water nitrogen cold, and we could riffle through the refrigerator, snoop around the pantry, and we could make our own sandwiches if we wanted, and we could put anything on them. Sarah's lips moved like she was saying a small prayer, the sky almost hued amber now, and it felt like a miracle, how this serene warmth had suddenly unfolded inside us and healed us faster than any old medicine.

We were under our beds, etching our names into the wood frames with a set of car keys we'd found behind a walk-in clinic. My sister etched, Sarah was alive, into her bed frame and I etched, Highway James ate here. The bottom of my mattress sagged and smelled like dead birds and I wondered if it was my smell or just something collected over the years. "Now we can go in peace," my sister said. We blew loose the wood shavings from our etchings and rolled out from under our beds and Martha was standing in the doorway with a book under her arm. "So you two found a home," she said. We tried to look up at her with calm eyes, caught in an act of defacement, about to leave the home, hopefully for forever, about to leave her, Martha, one of our many mothers, our brains collapsing because we didn't know what to say, didn't know how to put it into words, but Martha knew. She simply licked her finger and twisted off the turquoise ring she wore on her right thumb, a ring she wore every day, a ring I'd never seen her without, and set it on my sister's bed. Sarah shook her head like we wouldn't, couldn't accept it. "Just take it. Try to remember," Martha said, and I picked up the ring and put it in my pocket and sometimes you want to stay even though you know you should leave.

There was a haywire vending machine in the basement of a skyscraper downtown. All you had to do was press F5 or G7 and it would seize free snacks, Nutter Butters and 100 Grands respectively, and I'd stuff as many as would fit into my backpack. When they refilled the machine, which was every Friday or so, you could go back and do the same thing again, and even again, and there weren't any security cameras. At the home I sold the snacks to the kids for fifty cents off full price, the Nutter Butters going like hotcakes, and, after we'd found out we were going to a foster home, I took my nest egg from those sales to the theater on Randolph St. to buy a couple tickets. The theater was exquisite, the chipped brick facade, the neon sign running vertical down the side, and inside all stone and silver, with polished handrails winding up a marble staircase. The lady at the ticket counter shot me softhearted smiles as I piled my change and crumpled bills in front of her. "It's a wonderful performance. I saw it last Saturday," she said and handed me the tickets. It was all for Sammy. She'd almost turned downright phantasmal since she heard Sarah and I were leaving, locked away in her room, absent from everything, but when I slid those tickets under her door she must've felt some kind of old stirring love, because she unlocked almost immediately, her bedroom a tossed cave. "We probably won't ever see each other again. It's a shame," she said, and she was right, but we still had a little more music left.

The theater was a blitz of light and shadow and the violins were perfect. We were sitting middle-center, surrounded by perfumes and regalia, by people who probably gave charity money to the home. Sammy was wearing her best blouse, a red silk drape with three buttons on the front, her shoulders looking soft and strong, her eyes these curses. Everything she said was wonderfully poetic and she seemed happy. "It's like the longest dream I've ever had. And the man next to me smells like black leather," she said. I dressed up too, borrowing a slick pair of pinstriped slacks from Sal at the home. There was a rip right under the knee, but the slacks were baggy so the fabric folded over to cover my bare skin. Soon the conductor appeared on stage, the tail of his tuxedo jacket a long feather, and bowed, the crowd gently applauding. His spine went straight and he turned on a dime to face the orchestra and there was this beautiful quiet before he lifted his arms and the musicians began slowly moving on their instruments. We touched hands, Sammy and I, sitting there, dressed better than any commercial, feeling like we owned the core of the earth, and the violins swelled, and between the violins, a piano played a winged treble, and we could hear every note, like the keys were birthed perfectly between the strings, and soon what sounded like an ocean of cellos crawled along in dark tones. The spotlight switched to a fiberglass blue and the whole theater went tranquil in sound and shape and I looked over at Sammy's face, at those cursed eyes, and I really hope I never forget them.

Sally used all her techniques to try and calm Sarah – distraction, interruption, empathy, vanity. "You are so strong-willed, and that is such an important trait to have, but you have to know when to use it," Sally said. She also tried the techniques of bribery, blackmail, food, and finally anger. "You can't be in the hallway, Sarah, or the bathroom, or the dining room, or any other damn room besides this bedroom after lights out." Both of them, my sister and Sally, walked around with clenched fists for the final week we were there. Sarah wasn't sleeping, and because she'd been remanded to the bedroom, she played with a deck of cards all night, shuffling and reshuffling them on her bed, snapping them against the mattress, sorting them into piles, columns, and stacks until the sun rose. It was all a protest to get our birth mother to come back before we got a new mother, to get her attention again, to get her to realize the mistake she'd made, as though there was a world where we could be a family again. It was a misplaced rebellion, but I never said a word to my sister, because Sarah and our mother understood each other in a way I never did, like they were the same soul at different points in time, like my sister was looking at her future when she'd looked at our mother. I remember, when we were younger, they'd sleep in the same bed every night, in the only bedroom in the apartment, me in a makeshift crib on the sofa in the living room, the cushions built around me like a collapsing castle, and sometimes, after I learned to walk, and I could roam around in the darkness, I'd wander into the bedroom and watch them. They never seemed to be breathing, pressed together in perfect quiet, asleep, the streetlight shining through the half-opened window, a dog in the distance.

The second night we were in the foster home our foster father baked chicken and made mashed potatoes and we ate dinner in front of the TV, watching a movie about the end of the world, about an oiled pulse. Our foster mother almost choked to death on a chicken bone when she tried to make a comment about one of the actors with her mouth full. She started pounding her chest, trying to breathe, her eyes tearing up and her face turning blue, our foster father about to wrap his arms around her to perform the Heimlich, but suddenly she spat up a sliver of bone. "Good thing one of you kids didn't get that," she said, still breathing heavily. "Better me than you." We could almost see ourselves loving them. Our foster mother fell asleep halfway through the movie and woke at the end, asking what had happened, asking if all the people were safe, and our foster father told her that a few people had got offed. He locked the front door and we got ready for bed, brushing our teeth and running our mouths under the bathroom faucet to feel the pure cold water on our tongues. The apartment was tepid even at night and our foster father came and tucked us in. He knelt by the side of my bed and asked me if there was anything I needed and I said I didn't need anything. He turned off the light and left the door open a crack and I heard him walk down the hallway in slow, soft steps to my sister's room, where he asked her a couple questions and then said, "Don't hesitate about anything." I slept like a full wolf and in the morning our foster father had already left for work and our foster mother was in the kitchen, listening to the small radio on the counter and dancing while she made breakfast. It was bacon and eggs.

There was a drained wineglass on the kitchen counter and the apartment was hot, smelling all August like tangled bodies. Our foster mother stood at the kitchen sink and rinsed off a pair of scissors while she danced a samba. The L went by and the radio cut out for a minute and in the sudden quiet the apartment felt like an empty and burning museum. I was her morbid experiment, sitting on a stool in the middle of the kitchen with my head through a hole in a bedsheet. My sister stood in the kitchen doorway, her t-shirt torn away at her bellybutton, exposing a bruise near her hip. The radio came back on to a jazz ballad, to hi-hats and upright bass, and our foster mother snapped one eye shut for concentration and walked circles around me to the beat, tapping the scissors against the palm of her hand in time with the snares. She checked me from all angles, even leaning in close to compare my sideburns, snipping a couple more times at the sides to make sure they were perfectly blended. My sister was next. "I'm saving money for the real thing," Sarah said. Our foster mother poured another glass of wine and rinsed the scissors under the sink, leaving the faucet on for me, and I stuck my head under the warm water, my neck a spasm, the splinters of newly cut hair sticking to everything. "Your mother must've been a beautiful woman. Look at you two," our foster mother said. She danced over to my sister and brushed the hair out of Sarah's face and promised to keep it long enough to cover her ear.

"We used to hang around this street sometimes. I think I found my penknife in a car right over there. Now we live here," my sister said. It was the morning commute, the city cracking open. A semi-truck with a cartoon cow on the side shook the street, a man down the block yelled at someone like he was owed something, and a woman, one of our new neighbors, came out of the apartment building next door and walked up the street with an envelope in her hand. She wore a leather jacket and a helicopter seed was stuck in her hair. We nodded at her on her way back from the mailbox and she stood there for a long time, staring at us, her teeth manicured and skin smooth. My sister got up to pluck the seed from her hair, but the woman backed away, her panic visible. "This is a family neighborhood," she said and walked back to her apartment building, sweeping the seed away before she went inside. My sister pointed across the street, and in the front yard of one of the single-family homes, a man was digging a hole in the ground with a shovel for some reason. He was wearing a Cubs hat and a dress shirt and he must have felt our eyes on him, because he paused his digging to inspect us.

My sister sniffed her coat again for traces of cigarettes, unlocked the main door to our new building, and we snuck up the narrow stairwell, stopping outside each apartment door to listen to what was going on inside, but we only heard TVs or radios, no new violence. The building was old and hollowed out, with deep cuts in the walls from decades of moved furniture and a layer of skin dust on every surface. There were two apartments per floor, with three floors total, and at the top of the winding, wooden staircase our foster mother was standing on the landing. She was talking to a young woman, our neighbor, Maggie. The door to Maggie's apartment was halfway open and inside her stereo played thump techno and there were a bunch of empty drinking glasses on the coffee table and windowsill. When our foster mother introduced us, Maggie said welcome to the building, that it definitely has a history, and then she told us a story about a woman, a retired judge, who'd lived in that building her entire life, in the same apartment, who'd been born and had died in that apartment, on the second floor, directly below Maggie's. "She smoked probably four packs a day in there for fifty years and when they pulled up my kitchen floor to replace it the underside of the linoleum was all stained with cigarette smoke. It somehow got through the ceiling," Maggie said. Our foster mother said how disgusting, how gross, and my sister smelled her coat again and then snuck by us on the landing and went inside to the bathroom to wash her hands, soap her hair, brush her teeth, and spray perfume all over her coat, her usual system. When Sarah reappeared, I was in the living room with our foster mother. She was asking me questions about my sister while she dusted the bookcase and Sarah stood there, her hands in her pockets, staring ultraviolets at me, like now, James, with a family, we really need to hide who we are.

In the kitchen, there was a junk drawer full of loose parts and we riffled through it, hoping not to wake our foster mother from her afternoon nap. We finally found a bolt that might fit and then went outside and set the bike on its side and unscrewed the back tire. The original bolt was stripped smooth, and my sister screwed on the new bolt and we lifted the bike and rolled it back and forth on the sidewalk to make sure the wheel wouldn't fall off. It was a clean dream, a red Huffy we'd bought from a kid down the street for basically pennies. My sister hopped on and sped off downhill, her hair twisting around her face, looking like a punk rock rebel, with knee rips in her jeans from crashing over some factory fence and a bike helmet she'd spray-painted with loose symbols of anarchy. At the bottom of the street, she moved her feet to the back pegs, stood high on the bike, and coasted cleanly around the corner. I waited outside our building, imagining the tricks I'd do, some crank flips and bar spins, but Sarah didn't come back. I must've waited out there all afternoon, pulling up grass and walking around the block a couple times and talking to a neighbor, an airplane pilot, about drag and thrust, and finally, at dusk, my sister came pedaling up the hill. "I don't care if you don't believe me. I was lost," she said. We locked the bike to a fence behind our apartment building and hung out in the alley for a while, my sister in the shadows, leaning against a brick wall and smoking, telling me how she was never going to be famous.

After school our foster father took us to the lakefront, where we sat on a bench near the bike path and looked for flaws. It was Sarah's wild idea. "Everybody has something wrong with them. That's human," our foster father said to her. We saw a man with a single finger on his hand, a little boy in a wheelchair with thin curved legs, and a woman with a scar from cleft lip surgery. Our foster father opened the small red cooler he'd brought along and dug through the ice cubes and gave us each an orange juice. "That woman speaks through her neck. A tracheotomy," he said. The wind swirled off the lake, the sun a fading crescent, and I closed my eyes and drank my orange juice. We heard sirens somewhere behind us and our foster father said a small prayer for the person in the ambulance, like he always did. When I finished my orange juice I gave the empty bottle to my sister to throw away. She liked to look in trashcans for hideous things, recently finding a dead snake curled around an empty liquor bottle. Some boombox kids began to set up shop adjacent to the bench, so we took the L back to the apartment, where our foster mother was already asleep in her bedroom, the small TV on the dresser at a low drone. Sarah and I sat on the floor, on the rug at the foot of their bed, and watched a sitcom while our foster father washed up, changed into his pajama bottoms, and climbed into bed with his wife.

The walls of our apartment had been covered with three different kinds of wallpaper in four days, our birth mother a disintegrating asteroid, dressed in a strange black cloak she'd found somewhere, probably in a church basement, her hands covered in glue and ink and her favorite musician, Tim Buckley, continuously on blast throughout the apartment, the greetings album. In the dining room, a panel of blood-red wallpaper hung halfway down the wall, the top still unglued. My sister used a stepladder to climb up and glue the wallpaper to the top corner, but when Sarah got the panel smooth and perfect, our mother reached up and tore it down. We all laughed like dead clowns, lightheaded from the fumes, and our mother told us to keep working, to rehang the wallpaper she'd just destroyed. I was maybe five or six and skinny and my sister lifted me by the armpits so I could smear glue on the wall, and I remember the house phone rang and our mother turned down the stereo and ran to answer, a cigarette between her lips. She picked up the phone, listened for a long time, and then began screaming like the world was forever. She threw the phone against the cupboard and it busted open, the ringer sliding across the kitchen floor, and then she disappeared down the back stairwell of the building, yelling to us, "I'm going to see a dog about a man. No trouble," and my sister and I just kept hanging wallpaper.

The mechanic down the street, our neighbor, Jimmy, had a smooth Camaro, all white with black trim, leather seats, and a sunroof. For the past few months, he'd been down on his luck, his shop nearly closing after his divorce, his wife and son gone. Rumor had it that he was losing his marbles, all his oxbloods and aggies, and my sister and I often spotted him outside, in a lawn chair on his porch, in sweatpants, unshaven, with a pint of something clear at his feet. One October, when we were roaming around, following rich vagrants along side streets, getting some energy out before winter, we saw Jimmy outside, asleep in his chair in the cold, curled up and shivering, from wind or booze or both. My sister snuck up to him with quiet steps and pressed her hand against his forehead, but Jimmy didn't stir a centimeter. I asked her if he was dead, thinking about his son, but Sarah said he was still breathing, barely. "He's trying to find the void, but it's not that easy," she said. She checked his pulse, flicked his nose, and shook him like there was an intruder in the house, like it was time to get the baseball bat and get downstairs, and Jimmy's eyes slowly opened. It took him a long time to come to, but when he figured out what was happening, he leaned in and said something to my sister, something I couldn't hear. Later she'd tell me that he'd imparted a single sentence philosophy of life, and from that day forward, when Jimmy cruised down the street in his Camaro and happened to see us outside, he'd honk his horn and stick his hand up through the sunroof to give us the peace sign.

The movie was meticulously furnished, an explicit classic. Sarah and I were on the couch trying to watch, but our foster mother was in the kitchen with the sink full blast, doing dishes, singing one of her Irish ballads, and the sound of her singing and the water overpowered the voices of the actors. "And all the sweethearts I ever had, they'd wish me one more day to stay." She finally finished the dishes, wished us a goodnight, and went to her bedroom, where our foster father was feverish. The movie was about a hardened kind of object love, about proper value, with silken surfaces and shots through warped windows, but soon Sarah said she wasn't interested and turned off the TV. She went to the window to watch the storm, the snowflakes spinning like severed hands in the streetlight, and suddenly I felt like I was actually living alive, with the gunmetal light of the room, my sister as architecture, her hair tucked behind her ear, her ear itself, the bookcase in the corner, with worn books toppled over and scattered, the murmur of traffic down Western, our foster parents a soft layer if tragedy befell, so beautiful I seemed resuscitated. Sarah came back to the couch and pulled the blanket around us and moved closer so she could rest her head on my shoulder, telling me to twist a few of her fingers sideways until they cracked, and maybe it was all too serendipitous.

Our foster mother wore a black dress and our foster father a grey suit. They looked like a pioneer gold rush, a tactile mythology. We were in a small Italian restaurant on the near northside, eating at a table next to a window with lace curtains, the street frozen dark outside. My sister held her hand over the candle on the table, trying not to pull away even though it burned, which was a scene from her favorite film. I unfolded my napkin, my fork dropping to the ground, and when I bent under the table I saw our foster mother's feet crushed in her black shoes, and how her legs curved under the fabric of her dress, and I saw our foster father holding her hand, and how worn his suit actually was, the stitches loose along the seams, the cuffs unraveling above his shoes. I grabbed the fork and sat back up and our foster father said, "It's been a beautiful six months and we love you both. You're our pride and joy." My sister and I didn't know what to say, or how to say it, so we didn't say anything, and I remember how our silence felt like a violence.

A scurvy-looking rabbit was eating spring grass next to a chain-link fence in an empty lot a few blocks from our apartment, our foster father putting his finger to his lips to whisper, "Don't move or you'll scare it into the street." The rabbit lingered along the fence, its nose a siphon twitching, and our foster father pointed to the telephone wire, to a squirrel walking the line above. The rabbit glanced up and saw the squirrel and the squirrel looked down and saw the rabbit. Our foster father kept touching something on his neck and his face was agony when he pressed under his jaw. I think he knew that I already knew, and on our walk home he asked if I had a plan for my future, if I had anything in mind. "It's important to look ahead, but not lose sight. And to look back, but don't drown. It's important to be careful," he said. We stopped at a sandwich shop, but he didn't order anything, and we sat at a table in the back. The rugged fluorescents showed the scars on both our faces, and as he watched me eat I remember he called me son and explained what just another day at work felt like and how to survive that feeling.

We sat on the front steps of our apartment building and watched our neighbor go wild in the street. He was a pilot for a big airline. He didn't have a shirt on. There were scratches on his chest and neck and his elbows were bleeding. "Blood is swirling around his arm like one of those barbershop poles," my sister said. The pilot paced up and down the street, talking to himself, punching the air, kicking parked cars. He screamed toward the sky and then stuck his hand down his pants and began to dance a jig and the door to our apartment building flew open and our foster mother burst out, a small machine rushing across the street, ready to pounce. The pilot immediately cowered to the ground, afraid of her, and crawled along the gutter like a dying dog, small pieces of asphalt and rocks stuck to the bare skin of his back. He curled up with his face against the curb and our foster mother stood over him silently. He started to unbuckle his belt and when he got his belt all the way off he wrapped it around his neck and tightened, one notch at a time. "I heard what happened, Tom. Don't you go destroying yourself," our foster mother said. The pilot stared up at her, squinting his eyes in the sun, and we heard the ice cream truck a couple blocks away.

We were kicking a decrepit tennis ball down the street, the ball sliced open at the seam with pebbles jangling around inside. "Something's wrong with him. I can feel it," my sister said. It was the evening commute and the city was a broken clavicle, with church bells echoing off buildings and shards of green glass from shattered bottles on the sidewalk and crowds waiting on the corners to cross. My sister kicked the tennis ball into the middle of a busy intersection, where it bounced off the windshield of a car and ricocheted through the air. "The other day I was watching him and he didn't eat anything," she said. When we finally decided to go home, the apartment was dark and smelled like dried sap and we sat at the kitchen table and ate cereal straight from the box and waited for our foster father to come out of the bedroom. Soon enough he clicked on the kitchen light, his eyes alien, almost colorless, and sat gingerly at the table. Our foster mother appeared from the bedroom, still in her nightgown, not bothering to get fully dressed since the Sunday before. He swallowed a couple times, like what he was about to say was a lonesome stone in his throat. The window above the sink was open and we could hear some neighborhood kids playing outside. "I found something in my neck while I was shaving. It's not good," he said. His hands shook, and our foster mother, leaning there against the countertop, her lip twitched.

Her candle smelled like feral vanilla and the stereo on her dresser played Nirvana, the open window in her room looking straight into the window of the apartment next door, where some hanging plants were dead in their pots. Sarah unzipped her backpack, took out a pen and notebook, opened to a blank page, and put the pen between her teeth. "With our, with our, with our, what?" she said. Our foster mother and father were asleep in their bedroom, the ceiling above them probably peeling away like diseased paper, the white paint stained crimson-brown where he was breathing out whatever grew inside him. "With our everything changing forever," I said, but my sister didn't write it down. She just sat cross-legged on the bed and stared at the blank page. "With our everything gone," she said and wrote it down. I knew those coming days would be spiders, with a quiet crawling in through the cracks and burrowing inside us, the knocks on the front door just vibrations, all of us hidden away in our webs, circling the walls. Sarah finished her poem, and after I read it, I couldn't help but think we were cocooned.

Sarah said she was born blue. She said she remembered how she was covered in what came from of our mother, how those fluids were so warm, how the doctor shook and shook her to get her breathing, and how she was trying as hard as she could, but she just couldn't get any air. She said in that hospital room, our mother calmly asked for her baby, and then holding her close, pressed the palm of her hand against my sister's lungs and said, breathe, baby, breathe. My sister said was fighting so hard, so hard to live, but she was still floating through some different world, the world before this one, and our mother put her lips between my sister's eyes and kissed her there, whispering something she should never forget, and my sister finally took her first breath. "But I forgot what she whispered," Sarah said, stomping out her cigarette and slipping on her new pair of sunglasses, the street sunlit and boiling. I asked her what exactly had happened to our mother, what had caused her splits, her disappearances, and my sister grabbed my wrist and dug her nails in. "It's us. We're cursed with it. And now he's dying too," she said.

Outside the corner store a block up, where Sarah had stopped to buy a carton of milk, we bumped into the twins from the neighborhood. One of the twins said he'd just witnessed the wind hurl a metal trashcan onto the roof of a seven-story apartment building, and his brother confirmed his story, saying it was wild, that it looked like an Iraqi missile. They told us they were going down to the Amtrak tracks behind the bowling alley to light off some bottle rockets, to watch what this psycho wind would do to them, and asked if we wanted to go, but my sister wasn't interested, so she and I walked to the abandoned lot a few blocks from our apartment, the lot where I'd saw the rabbit and the squirrel with our foster father. Newspaper and fast-food wrappers were caught in the chain-link fence, flapping in the wind, and my sister bit off the top the milk carton, spit the chunk of cardboard on the ground, put her mouth around the hole, bent her head back, and drank, the milk like bone waves going down her throat. We sat against the fence for half an hour and tried to smoke in the windstorm and I remember she took my hand and, without looking at me, slid it under her hoodie to press it against her bare skin and hold it there, but to feel her heartbeat only.

There was a leaf in the gutter shaped like a handprint and the street sweeper was only a couple blocks up. My sister unzipped her backpack to get out a fresh pack of cigarettes, squinting to see across the street to the church. She bit open the pack, the cellophane sticking to her lips for a second, put two cigarettes in her mouth, cupped her hands, lit them, and handed one to me. The sky had been mars maroon all afternoon and the wind was cold, but I felt good, like the oiled gears of a clock or maybe the talon of a bird. "I've been seeing and hearing things," Sarah said. "Like goddamn things that I don't think exist, or should exist. Like blurred people in the corners of my bedroom and eyes and mouths in the tops of trees and people screaming at me as I try to fall asleep." She flicked her cigarette at a parked car, and we walked across the street to the church, where the front door was scuffed wood etched with doves, and inside it was quiet, with a few candles burning. We stood near the back pews for a long time, our pupils growing in the darkness, the stained glass windows becoming reds and blues across the altar. There was a man up front, on his knees, with his head bowed, praying. My sister whispered something in my ear and I could smell the smoke in her hair, and we walked down the aisle, our footsteps echoing off the stone floor, the stations moving down the sidewalls. As we walked closer, we could hear the man's prayer, hear what he really wanted, and Sarah and I lost all shape, all sense, because we wanted the exact same thing for our foster father, but we also wanted to never need to pray.

Our foster father was the outline of something stealth. He sat in his favorite chair in front of the TV and ate a peanut butter and jelly sandwich. Earlier in the week the doctors had checked his neck, armpits, his lungs, scheduled a biopsy, and told him to stay resilient, that there were positive percentages. He wasn't moving the same, though, like his body was already a shell. Every bite he took of his sandwich was slow and calculated and he chewed forever, to the point that what was in his mouth had to be mush. Our foster mother sat on the couch and watched TV with him, all nerves, sitting on her hands, addressing him without looking. "I bought a new jar of honey. It's in the cupboard," she said. During the commercial break, he stood from his chair and started to move toward the kitchen, toward the cupboard, but then he stopped, and his head sunk into his chest, and he rested there, leaning in the doorway, with his hand against the wall, breathing heavily, unnaturally. He finally raised his head with all he had and said, "I'm not really in the mood for honey, honey."

Her hands were cut up from more barbed wire, from jumping a jobsite fence and stealing a box of tools, but she said she was sleeping better now. As we walked to the grocery store, she recounted a story in that morning's newspaper, where, in the next neighborhood over, a single-family home had been torched, a suspected arson, and a family of five had died. They hadn't released the names of the dead yet. "Why do they need to notify the family first? If someone dies we should know as fast as possible," my sister said. I grabbed an abandoned shopping cart from the sidewalk and pushed it down the street and into the store. The air conditioning hummed, the cold air bliss, and we went directly to the magazine aisle, where we sat on the floor and gathered magazines in piles around us. We loitered there for an hour, reading about new TV shows and the President's dog and the Olympics in Atlanta, even though a woman who worked at the store had warned us about just sitting and reading and not buying. My sister showed me a picture of a squid in a nature magazine and read the caption underneath. "Three hearts and eight arms and two tentacles and curved claws on the suction cups," she said. Static came from the ceiling speakers, an announcement of inventory, and I turned the magazine I was reading sideways and the woman on the page had ribs like teeth.

The sun had been rattling everything all day. The telephone wires were bare of birds and all the dogs in the neighborhood were hiding quiet in the shade. Our foster mother pulled her long t-shirt over her head and underneath her swimsuit was stars and stripes. There was a long scar down the side of her leg, a bicycle accident from when she was a girl, she said. She laid out her towel on the small patch of grass in front of our building, clicked open a bottle of sunscreen, and squirted some on her hands, rubbing them together in a peculiar way, like you would with perfume. She rubbed sunscreen along her neck and all down her legs and on her feet, and I heard a voice above me and looked up and Sarah's head was sticking out of our third-story window. She was yelling something down, but I couldn't hear, or pretended I didn't hear, and soon she was down there with her towel too, spreading it out next to our foster mother, taking off her sundress, the tattoo on her stomach still brand new, the skin around her bellybutton peeling. I read the cursive of her tattoo again and it said something about children.

There were a couple cops at the Italian beef stand. One of them, a cop with a thin face and sideburns, I recognized from somewhere, maybe from the time we were outside the hospital with that kid and his gun. When they got their sandwiches, they went to their cruiser to eat, and I signaled to my sister in the alley and she unzipped her backpack and got out her spray cans. From the corner, I monitored the gumshoes, the windows of their cruiser cracked open, the battering ram on the front, a head-sized dent in the door. My sister tied a black bandanna around her neck and mouth, hiding everything except her eyes, and switched spray cans like she was programming drums, her idols always elsewhere when she painted. The thin-faced cop tossed his second sandwich wrapper out the window and the cruiser revved its engine and I screeched our signal, a jacked-up bird call, and my sister packed up her cans, tossed her backpack over her shoulder, and ran from the alley. The cops drove straight down there, of course, right past me feigning innocence on the corner, and crept along in an indelicate performance. They came to a complete stop in front of Sarah's graffiti, idling there for what seemed like a summer day, but then finally moved along, taking a left turn from the alley onto Lincoln. With the cops officially gone, I went down to look and she'd painted a grisly, armored creature, maybe an armadillo, with ammunition.

Sarah held her liberated thumbnail up to the sun. There were small river grooves on the underside and it was shaped like a miniature moon. She gave me the pocketknife and I slid open the sharpest blade and put it against my finger. "You said if I did, you'd do it. It's time to show what you're capable of," she said. I took a deep breath and began to cut around my thumbnail, sawing the skin a little at a time. Blood pooled around my cuticle and I slid the blade of the knife between the nail and the nail bed and leveraged up hard and my thumbnail popped horizontal, only held on by a bit of skin. I dropped the knife in the alley and grabbed hold of my nail and like a tooth twisted it off. On a discarded couch next to a dumpster, we compared the size and shape of our thumbnails, mine more baseball field to her moon, laughing at what we'd just done to ourselves, my sister pushing down on the fresh, exposed skin to dirty it up.

I went to the kitchen for a glass of water and our foster mother had her head down on the table. I wanted to let her rest, so I gently opened the cupboard, got out a clean glass, and softly ran the kitchen sink. She spoke without lifting her head, just loud enough that I could hear over the sound of the water. "There are things we can't do anything about," she said. From the window above the sink, she'd seen the years. She'd seen kids fist fight for honor, neighbors walk home from work like caged sloths, cracks in the sidewalks grow, potholes cave, Jimmy, the mechanic, drink and recover, Tom, the pilot, breakdown and disappear, cops dispatched in droves, fire trucks catch fire, and, of course, the ambulances. "My mom died alone in her bed in a too-hot room on the top floor of her apartment building with no money, two dresses to her name, and maybe a little jewelry. My brother and I went to save that bed after her death, a handcrafted bed, the same bed you sleep in now," she said. I pulled the curtain closed, chugged my water, put the dirty glass in the sink, and said goodnight, but in bed I was paralyzed, running my finger without a nail along the carved wooden frame, listening to nighttime delivery trucks crater up Western, and a door opened, and then a door closed, and I rolled to my side, faced the wall, and tried fall asleep so I might wake without past or future.

There were dirty dishes piled in the sink with grease stuck to them in streaks. All of us were at the kitchen table, our foster mother dealing a deck of cards and our foster father sitting slumped in his chair, exhausted from his surgery. My sister asked him to see it again and he loosened the bandage on his neck, folded it back, and showed us the couple stitches, the catgut threads. "It's not really that bad. We all have a little something growing inside us. Remember that," he said. Our foster mother dealt the last of the cards and drank her wine. She was a bluebird in that low kitchen light, with her plum skin and flint eyes. "Just call. I got zilch," she said, sliding her cards facedown on the table. "Finally, some luck," our foster father said and snapped his cards over. He beat us with hearts and queens. A dish shifted in the sink and we could already feel the looming Chicago winter reshaping everything, the apartment beginning to growl, the wooden doors contracting, the sink in the bathroom draining like slush, the frigid kitchen linoleum sticking to our bare feet. Our father said he was too tired for another game, did his goodnights, and then went down the hallway to the bedroom. Our foster mother packed up the playing cards and my sister and I went to the living room to watch TV on the couch, where we wrapped a blanket around us, Sarah putting her feet in my lap, telling me to crack her toes, and I twisted them one by one until even her pinkies cracked.

The older man who lived in an apartment on the first floor invited me inside after I asked him how he was feeling, our foster mother telling us he'd had a small stroke. His apartment was another vestibule, with everything giving off a dust mite smell. On the coffee table, there were thin strips of red, raw meat laid out on paper towels and a clear plastic bowl of dark liquid. The man leaned forward and picked up a strip of meat and then dipped the strip into the bowl. "Dip it. Dry it. And you got jerky. Last you the winter," he said. He went to the kitchen and came back with two non-alcoholic beers, telling me to have a seat on the couch, which was covered in a floral bed sheet. Across the room, there was a tarnished piano in the corner, a divine, curved amoeba in the gloomy light. "I used to play, the blues," he said, taking a sip of beer and nodding for me to do the same. I did and it tasted good. I took a couple more sips, eased back on the couch, stretched my legs out, and studied the piano and the photo of a woman that sat atop the fallboard. The photo was black and white and scrawled across the bottom, in what looked like thin lipstick, was a message in red writing. The man followed my eyes and we looked at the picture together. "That one," he finally said. "That one was the one right there. She could really play. I messed it up good though." He took a sip of his beer and stretched out his legs too. "You got a love?" he said. "Really think now, son. I'm talking about that different kind of love."

A section of waterlogged newspaper was wrapped around the antenna of a parked car, the ink bleeding in the rain. My sister and I huddled against the side door of a closed tavern in the mouth of an alley and watched traffic. Sarah's hair was soaked, smashed to her forehead, and she pulled the hood of her sweatshirt tighter, rain dripping off the tip of her nose. "Did I ever tell you that our mother thought she had bad blood in her? Like our grandfather had been a murderer, or his father, or something like that. She was obsessed with it. Like you with war," she said. The rain eased for a moment, the cars creeping along with their windshield wipers squeaking, and we pulled ourselves up from the doorway and walked a deserted block or two to an emergency clinic, where we ducked under the overhang of the patient loading zone. My sister grabbed a can of spray paint from her backpack and I looked out for cops. I nodded the all-clear and she started to paint the brick. She said painted what she needed to see, but never saw – animals with hundreds of tails, women with fire for fingernails, forms of obsolete currency, a ten kilometer comet.

One midnight, when we were eating cereal at the kitchen table, attempting to crunch quietly and not clang our spoons against the bowls and wake them, our foster father came out of the bedroom, got a bowl and spoon for himself, and sat with us. He was beginning to look imperfectly reborn, his hands steadying like he was ready to fight rabid. He watched my sister stencil something in her milk with her spoon, something that disappeared as soon as the milk went smooth again, a portrait of a man with a fresh spear or the first second of a long night's sleep, depending on the cancer. "I'm going to need you to be there when I need you to be there. Down the road," she said, looking him straight in the eye. And he understood what we were pushing home, what we spelled shining for him in every dark we could, what we hoped heavy, but he just stared at me from across the table, a signal that I would be the last and only fix for her future needs, because he also understood his body.

He came back from chemo and slept for two days straight. Lymph nodes and he took some painkillers, but after a while the medicine would wear off, and then lymph nodes again. Our foster mother walked around the apartment with a screwdriver clutched in her hand like a knife. She took apart anything with screws – tables, chairs, clocks, drawers, the door hinges, the typewriter. She hoped our foster father would put them back together again, eventually. My sister started to hide anything that could be dismantled, like the toaster in the closet and a music box under the sink, until our foster mother calmed down enough to watch TV. She kept the screwdriver in her hand, though, poking the rusted head into her thigh during commercial breaks. Sarah watched her like satellites, like she had with our birth mother, but our foster mother never talked to any ancestral ghosts, never cut her arm open, never dropped roses to the snow, never disappeared underground, but the next morning, after she'd forced our foster father to drink a full glass of water and eat small slivers of an orange, our foster mother told us that in the middle of the night, while she was awake in bed and analyzing, she'd actually prayed for apocalyptic floods. Not a single flood, but floods.

The whites of his eyes were a snake pit of veins and I waited for one to slither out of his tear duct, drop to the table, and just crawl. "I don't want to fall apart slowly like my father did," he said. His voice was becoming a grating whisper, a melt inside his body, and to actually hear him we had to lean in close, which we did, even though he sometimes resisted the closeness. He swore his voice was still his voice, but he couldn't hear himself, couldn't register the change, so my sister taught him how to use her tape recorder and he spent at least an hour a day in his bedroom recording his voice, telling stories, mostly about Vietnam. He'd close the windows, turn off the lights, and talk about the cherries and the traps, the medic who refused to carry a gun, the GI who woke one morning and told the others exactly how he was going to die later that day, which came true. We played the tape back for him and he heard how his voice was different, how it was crumbling. His eyes welled up and he told us that from now on he was going to drink at least three cups of tea per day to keep his voice fresh. So most nights I'd sit at the kitchen table and drink tea with him, mainly mint, and like clockwork, because of the warmth and steam of the tea, our eyes would begin to close and we'd both say goodnight and drift off to our bedrooms like the exorcised, the apartment almost peaceful, and in the morning I'd often lay in bed, the sun crawling across the floor, or it would be overcast with no sun at all, and I'd imagine what the moment of death would feel like, what it will feel like to leave this all.

For a couple weeks my sister carried dead batteries around in her pocket. She hoped one would break open, leak acid through her jeans, and burn her leg. She wanted to feel something she'd never felt before, a charged sensation, something to stun her nerves. A waitress came over to our table and asked us if we wanted anything else. She was chewing gum and her tongue looked like a topographic map, with long, white, raised peaks. "Do we have anything left? Probably not much," my sister said, and I pulled our crumpled bills and junked up change from my pocket and arranged it on the table. Sarah twitched in her seat, digging her fingers inside her cup to slide an ice cube into her mouth and crack it between her teeth. I looked at the food I still had on my plate. The meat was pink and the fries were a mess. We didn't have enough for much else, so I put the money away and Sarah gasped and winced and one of the batteries slid from the burnt hole in her pocket and hit the floor, rolling out from under the table, slowly trailing acid across the diner, and the waitress, watching it roll, said she'd go in the back to get the baking soda like it was everyday normal.

There was a van with a wheelchair lift parked outside the VA and a man was being lowered down in his wheelchair. He clutched a stuffed lion to his chest and the skin of his face seemed see-through, showing his skull. A woman held the arm of the wheelchair as it was being lowered to make sure it didn't tip over. She looked at our foster father and then at me and smiled a small, sad smile. "I made it home, but I guess the war still got me," our foster father said. We climbed into his truck and left the hospital and drove circles around the city, finally pulling over outside an old theater, where we sat, idling, Sammy slipping into my mind. He took off his sunglasses and stared straight ahead, his eyes fractured in the early winter sun. "I can't remember what show we saw here, but I remember she told me afterwards that I had to get my shit together or I had no chance with her," he said. "So I got my shit together." Outside the theater, the whole scene, the small light bulbs framing the marquee, the red ceramic tiles of the roof, the descending sky, his eyes, his shaking hands, so thin, the scar on his neck, was like an exploding star. "If anyone you love ever needs you, no matter what, you be there," he said. "Even if you need you." He pulled away from the theater and drove north on the Dan Ryan while we listened to news radio, to Ebola virus hysteria, the spread of a disease, just like the one in him caused by Agent Orange.

It'd been a strange night, the apartment a pixelated dark, our foster father asleep in the bedroom, having finally finished an entire meal, a small steak and slice or two of potato, my sister somewhere out in the city, masquerading as royalty, our foster mother shuffling around on the couch, searching for the remote to turn on the TV, its flash cutting through the darkness. We watched a movie set in '68 Mississippi while she told me a story about how our foster father had taken her downtown on their second or third date, to dinner, and how they'd enjoyed a light meal and talked politics – Pan Am, Chernobyl – until the restaurant closed. She remembered how they used to be. "We really thought we had a chance to do something, but there's just too much money to overcome," she said, closing her eyes and resting her head against the armrest of the couch. And that was the first time I thought about the White House fence, and I think I wanted to wrap myself around her, around anybody I could, like a shield, as a sacrifice.

Our teacher, Mr. Nunez, who'd come back from Desert Storm, who walked with a hard limp, like his hipbone was jelly, wrote the names of WWI battles on the blackboard, circling each location and telling us how many people had died there. He looked at the numbers like they were family, like any loss was his loss. "Write at least a page about how the definition of basket case has changed over time. What does it mean now?" he said. I opened my notebook and imagined I was a soldier on a beach, with explosions thick around me. I didn't know where I was, or why, and the water was on fire and there were capsized and sinking ships on the horizon. I hadn't used my gun yet, didn't want to use my gun, so instead I dug deeper and deeper into the sand, into my foxhole, until everything except my open eyes and flaring nostrils was buried. After the battle, after the bodies were examined and dog tags catalogued, I trudged along the beach with the other ragged but alive soldiers, our faces caked with dried blood, sand, mud, the waves rushing up over our torn-apart boots, the salt getting through our socks, burning the cuts and sores on our feet. Then I imagined another war, and I was up in a tree, beating away mosquitos and watching a line of enemy soldiers march through the jungle. I was a sharpshooter, sniper. The wind smelled like skin and something shifted in the distant, tall grass so I steadied my gun and fired. And then I fired again.

Our foster father was freshly shaven, his hair combed and parted, but his cowlick was still giving him trouble, sticking up like a velvet antler. He seemed in strong spirits. His white dress shirt was pressed, and he was even wearing cufflinks, a turquoise pair in the shape of waning moons. He kissed our foster mother on the cheek as she sat at the kitchen table and took a few packages of mint tea from the box on top of the refrigerator and put them in his briefcase. He still wanted to work, to keep his mind about him, he said. I washed my cereal bowl and watched from the kitchen window as people assembled at the bus stop at the end of the street. Some of them were gathered in groups of two or three, maybe to keep warm, and some were alone, touching their faces or craning their necks around the corner in search of the bus. Soon our foster father was down there with them, because he never liked to drive to work, and I remember I wanted him to look up, to see me in the window, washing an already clean bowl, but he looked down at his hands, down at his shoes, down at the ground as though an alluring unknown was hidden just below the crust.

My sister was stretched out lengthwise on the couch, her legs on my lap, my hand on her hipbone. We watched a movie about regrets, waiting for our foster father to get home from work. About an hour later, he labored upstairs, stumbled inside, and dropped his briefcase next to his chair. "What channel is this? This is a classic," he said. Onscreen, a hard rain fell, drenching the street of some nondescript, black-and-white city, and a man, barely visible in a fog, leaned against a lamppost, his fedora hiding his eyes, raindrops dripping off the brim. With a deep, almost alien voice, the narrator began, "Sick inside, he stood in the rain that last midnight, looking into the window of the woman he loved, but a woman whom he'd never touch again; and with a faint light behind her, she stood there softly, her silhouette like sparks dragging, her fingers static, her pale eyes staring down into the rain, seeing him down there, on that empty street, that man, that dying husk, his hat covering his blistered face; and, no, she wasn't afraid of him, knowing who he truly was, knowing she was part of him, arising in his dreams, and in those last moments of himself, he wiped the rain from his brow, and my love, he thought, I will leave you now and forever and become something without you." The narration ended and in the next scene the man was on a train and our foster father got comfortable in his chair and told us to turn up the volume, my sister and I glancing at each other, understanding that we all might be that damned.

Our foster mother was wrapped in a white cotton robe, asleep on the couch, looking like watercolors, like a fading landscape. A slight sun was coming through the curtains and everything was shaded mint, her chest expanding with each breath, her eyes twitching under her eyelids. The TV was still on from the movie the night before and the morning news showed a story about a city junkyard, about a burned houseboat with remains inside. Our foster mother's eyes stopped twitching and she shuffled her body on the couch, turning her back to the TV. "Everything passes in time," she'd said a few nights ago, when I was worrying a hole in myself. We were at the kitchen table, under the soft bulb, dead bugs inside the ceramic fixture, and she'd leaned back in her chair, stretched her arms behind her head, rolled her wrists, yawned, and then said it like it was something true.

Mr. Nunez was teaching us about orbital nights, gravity and time, how we still may not be able to measure certain things properly, and one of the smaller girls in class, a girl with a mother in prison, raised her hand and said she wanted to be an astronaut. "Read as much as you can about it. A key when trying to understand anything," he said. The plastic window blinds in the classroom were open and it was a metallic day. Outside, my sister's class was on the baseball field with barometers, measuring the air. I watched her wander around by herself, shaking the barometer, her hair twisting around in the tough wind, flurries finding her shoulders. She looked like the skeleton of a preserved animal, with her long, gloved fingers, and soon she was out in centerfield talking to herself, really having a conversation, kicking frozen dirt and bucking her head around, but when I asked her about it later she said I was just seeing things, that I was imagining her mouth move.

Sarah was messing with a new knife she wouldn't tell me where she got, pushing the tip of it into her forehead until it left a purple crater. We were on the floor in her bedroom, trying to draw the perfect circle, but everything we did was a distorted oval and she was losing interest, the knife now against her stomach, underneath her tank top, against her sternum. Her bedroom had changed since the last time I'd been in there, with a gigantic wall poster of an abstract letter bomb hung above her headboard. There were no longer any photos of our mother on her dresser either, and the photo of us at the group home, a photo with about twelve of us taken one summer, was gone too. In that photo, my sister looked like a guerrilla, in her black boots and her face dirtied, and Sammy was wearing her Walkman and had a scab on her knee, and I, standing there between them, looked younger than I'd ever felt. "I'm done. I'm going to sleep," Sarah said and kicked off her shoes without untying them and I stacked our attempted circles and set the papers on her dresser, not daring to search inside her open top drawer for the photos.

The apartment smelled like sunflower and vinegar and our foster mother was in the bathroom with the door open a crack. She stood at the mirror, her eyes blue smoke and her face porcelain, her hair done up, with a couple twisted strands hanging down her neck, the strap of her black dress loose on her shoulder, a silver bracelet. "I laid your clothes out on your bed," she said, still concentrated on the mirror. There was an ironed white shirt, a pair of pressed black pants, a black tie on my bedspread, and I got dressed, buttoning my cuffs, but I couldn't tie a tie yet, and our foster father was sick in the bedroom, so I went to the bathroom with my collar up, the tie dangling around my neck. It only took her a couple attempts and I could smell her perfume, that sunflower, and I remember how we looked in that bathroom mirror, the two of us dressed like hardboiled noir. On the L, the sunset a horizontal helix, our foster mother tapped her high heel against the floor, the men pretending not to watch. We arrived at our stop and walked the couple blocks, past the chicken and feed building, to the school, where we went straight to the auditorium. It was already dark, and a whisper, cough, and Sarah walked out on stage and sucked everyone's eyes straight to her, the narrow shadows of her long bones suspended in the spotlight, a moray in oil, a fin almost erupting from her back, and our foster mother, so proud, grabbed my hand and together we watched my sister electrocute the opening monologue.

"A man was running down a side street as fast as he could, sucking air. He slipped in the snow, regained his balance, his limbs flailing, and then he slipped again. His eyes were as wide as eyes could get and his boots were untied and the pockets of his jeans were turned inside out. He was a doomed animal, prey, as he ran against traffic, crisscrossing the street to try and throw off their scent. Three police officers chased after him, one officer stopping to catch his breath, halting on the sidewalk and hunching to a knee in the snow. An entire night's breath burst from his mouth, and he stood again, unclipped his holster, drew his gun but didn't fire. He yelled something inaudible at the man and then radioed to the others. Soon there were sirens and gunshots and I drifted towards the sound of them, a few blocks south, and that same man lay on a sidewalk in front of a clothing store, crumpled in the snow, with his right arm slightly in the air, like he was reaching out for something. Two police cars were parked diagonally near where the man lay and the three officers surrounded him with guns drawn. The clothing store had an advertisement for jeans in the front window, and the model, a rippling, shirtless man, was displayed in a bed of thorns with what looked like the universe above him, a mural of space and stars, and the model seemed to be staring right down at the unfortunate man in the snow."

Our next-door neighbor, Maggie, buzzed me up and invited me inside to wait until my sister or someone got home. She had a half-assembled puzzle on the coffee table, a medieval death scene, with idealized figures committing heinous acts of violence. There was also a candle on the table, with snuffed out cigarettes inside, and she reached in for a refry, lit it, took a couple puffs, and then dropped the butt into her coffee cup, where it sizzled out. "So, how was school?" she said, bending down to search for something under the couch, pushing my feet aside, the couch worn and smelling like she'd been sleeping on it for years, a nested salt smell, with every part of it seemingly perpetually warm. I told her we'd mostly read about electricity and that I'd lost my apartment keys on the way home. She made a sound like a crippled horse and popped up from the floor, finding a full cigarette under the couch, which she then lit and walked over to the half-open, fogged window to blow the smoke outside. "Do you still have to dissect things?" she said. The stereo was notched high and the song that played sounded like ultra bubbles, with technological pulses and a mathematical voice, and I'd never heard anything like it before, so Maggie, seeing my reaction, went over and notched up the sound even more.

I hustled after Maggie through the falling snow, trying to stay stride for stride with her, but her legs were too long and liquid. She kept looking back, her black leather jacket zipped to her chin, her eyes narrow to keep out the snow. She finally stopped under the shelter of a bus stop to wait for me, the city so quiet around us, the aftermath of something nuclear. She was different than another mother. She wasted too much time with jumbled talk to care for anything seriously, but I had perfect the ears for that, and I liked the feeling that if I was born her crib I'd probably die. When we finally made it to the corner store, we walked the sparse aisles, shaking the ice from our hair, and after we'd warmed up, Maggie went to the counter and bought cigarettes and a fifth of vodka and paid for them with a few bills and some change. "I recognize your hands from somewhere. Did you get those callouses in my garden?" she said to the clerk. On the walk back to our building, it started snowing harder and Maggie stopped her gallop to stand in the middle of the sidewalk and look up at the gray, spiraling sky. "These are the spider-under-the-skin days. It'll get better," she said. She gulped some vodka and grabbed my hand, and I remember I wanted to pull apart every machine in the world by the wires just to hear what she'd say next.

The ceiling of the bar was embroidered golden farmland, the bartender with a dirty towel draped over his shoulder and a tattoo of a leopard on his forearm. Behind him were bottles on a back shelf, in front of a large mirror, and Maggie told him she needed tequila and pointed to the bottle she wanted. I watched her drink until her face warped silly. "You seem like a person with sink ships kind of lips. Your sister. Your sister might be the next Annie Oakley," she said. She pinched my knee to see if I was okay, if I was comfortable in an uncomfortable place, and then asked for another drink, the oil on her face thickening, her lips silently moving to the song on the jukebox. She drank for another hour and then we stumbled home, Maggie leaning into me for support. The light bulb in the hallway flickered and Maggie finally found her keys in her purse and pushed through her front door. She rubbed her stomach under her sweatshirt and hooked her fingers inside the beltloops of her jeans. "Everything is going wrong for me," she said. She lit a cigarette and together we sat on her windowsill and watched the city, the birds in bare trees, the quills of ice. Her pack was sitting on the windowsill and I grabbed a cigarette and lit it. "What an involved experiment this is. We should be applauded," she said with a quick slur to her speech and we smoked there at the window until she suggested something else.

My sister asked me why I'd been going over to Maggie's apartment so often. We were watching cartoons on the couch before school and the duck kept dying, his beak blowing out the back of his head. My sister was laughing and I thought she was laughing at the duck, but she was probably laughing at Maggie and me. Our foster father came out of the bedroom dressed for work, but after eating a breakfast of orange slices, he said he felt nauseous and went back to the bedroom. "You know she's a hardcore alcoholic or something. You're sixteen, James," Sarah said. I told her that Maggie had interesting music, that she spoke with a new flavor, that she was within reach. My sister went to her bedroom and came back with the photo of the twelve kids taken at the home, the one with guerilla Sarah and scabbed Sammy, and handed it to me. "Don't go diving into that girl. Trust me. Go find Sammy, if you need to. She knows how much something can hurt. She's one of us," Sarah said. The photo felt like it was eroding in my hand and my sister grabbed it back and propped it up on the bookcase in the living room, in the most prominent spot still available.

I drank the last of the milk on purpose, half a carton without stopping to breathe, so I had a reason to go next door. The hallway smelled like strange cooking, like spiced fur, and I could hear voices. I knocked on Maggie's door and some guy opened and leaned there smoking a cigarette, waiting for me to speak. He had burn holes in his white t-shirt and his hair was wet and he was barefoot. There was music playing inside, what sounded like a statistical opera, a ricochet of snares, and Maggie sat cross-legged on the couch in her bra and underwear. I stood at the door, trying to grasp the music, looking at the empty beer bottles scattered around the apartment, the bottle of tequila on the coffee table, looking at Maggie's legs and stomach, her bare shoulders, her breasts. "James, you're dressed in the finery of a Ferrari salesman," she said, her speech more twisted than usual, and I realized that girl was the option of a noose, a halfhearted crime, and for a second I hated my sister for being right, but that didn't last long, because she was my sister.

We were outside one night, during the tail end of winter, the neighborhood an expectant burn, a nervous stir for Spring, and a shooting star with a green bow shock split the sky, and when we turned our faces upward, I swore I felt stardust land on my forehead, on the bridge of my nose, in the corners of my mouth. It landed, dissolved strange for a split second, and then melted into my skin. Upstairs, our foster mother was probably cooking chicken in the kitchen and our foster father was probably in there with her. "You say that now, but we'll see, honey," he might've said. Through the kitchen window, they kept an eye on us, my sister still with her chin to the stars, sucking in new particles. When the chicken was done, our foster mother cracked the window open and called down in her famous whistle, like she always did, that high-pitched long rope, and we went upstairs for dinner. The four of us ate chicken at the kitchen table and our foster father asked Sarah, "What do you want for your eighteenth, old lady?" and our foster mother knifed a breast in half like she wanted to extinguish the question.

My sister and I took the L to the Chicago station and walked a couple blocks west to a corner bar with a wooden sign swinging over the door. There were two or three people inside, all men, all sitting at the bar watching a gameshow on a mounted TV. When the bartender, a woman with a pixie cut, saw my sister, she gave her a slight nod and pointed toward one of the booths at the rear of the bar, near the pool table. She poured one of the men something dark and then made her way over to us, a brown paper bag, stapled at the top, in her hand. "Just my brother," my sister said as she dug in her pocket and pulled out a small stack of folded bills, the outside bill a $20, and gave it to the bartender. The bartender counted the money as fast as she could and handed us the brown paper bag, and without saying another word, we left the bar, walked a couple storefronts down, my sister keeping the bag at her side, obviously hiding it, and ducked into an alley. Something smelled loose and rotted, the dumpster spilling over, thawing, and my sister opened the paper bag, looked inside, and from the look on her face, a sideways shine of pure menace, I could tell that whatever was supposed to be in the bag wasn't. She stormed back to the bar, but when Sarah tried to open the door, it was locked, so she shook the brass handle, banged her fist above the deadbolt, and then looked in the window. Some of the lights inside the bar had been turned off, but we could still see the bartender, serving a man a drink and laughing at a joke, and when the bartender saw us at the window she flashed a sinister smile, and my sister kicked at the door a bunch of times and we left, because it was only money.

I was awake all night, watching the moon cross the window, listening to a dog bark behind our building. The neighbors kept him, a blue speckled heeler, chained to a metal post pounded into the dirt in their backyard. They were a wobbly young couple, barely able to dress themselves, always wearing soiled sweatpants and old flannel shirts. Drugs, some said, and freeing that dog had been the talk of the neighborhood for a long time, but nobody had done anything yet. Most nights I listened to him bark angry, fearful, chopping barks, coughing barks, until the barks, eventually, when the dog realized he was on his own, changed to lonely howls after midnight. When the sun began to rise, my body feeling like a long scratch, I rolled out of bed, pulled open the curtain, and looked for the dog. He was asleep on the dirt, curled into a ball like a fox, his paw over his face, and I watched him for a while to make sure he was breathing. Everybody in the apartment was still asleep so I tiptoed to the kitchen and grabbed some strawberries from the fridge and then went to the living room to watch TV on mute. It was Sunday morning, and everything was about God. I finished the strawberries and turned off the TV and shuffled down the hallway to my sister's room and cracked open the door. She was lying on her back, wrapped in her blanket, her forearm on her forehead, covering her face.

Our foster mother wore a pair of yellow rubber gloves and scrubbed the dishes as hard as she could, the kitchen splattered with salmon oil and potato grease from dinner, the radio on the counter on the news. I opened my history book to a picture of a Panzer, of Geronimo, of a bread line, of the Apollo mission, and tried to buckle down. Water splashed up from the sink and she wiped her forehead with her forearm. "Where's your sister, anyway?" she said. Probably living some invented desire, on the L, with a scheme in her head and a small knife in her pocket. And I think Sarah and our foster mother both recognized the divisions, the divide between the sea and mountains, us always the sea, tirelessly sweeping the debris, them the mountains, and she turned off the radio, the faucet, and asked me what I was reading, but I told her I was only thinking, and when she asked me what I was thinking about, I said the natural world, and she said sometimes the world doesn't feel so natural, does it?

The bed of our foster father's truck was packed with towels and blankets, folding chairs and jugs of water, my sister sitting back there as we drove, screaming every time he sped up, the warming wind sucking back her face like an astronaut. We'd all made it through winter and he said he was feeling better. We got to Montrose Beach and unpacked the truck and walked toward the water. Our foster father bent down to scoop up a handful of sand and put it in his back pocket. "I bet one day someone will count every grain of sand on earth," he said, already barefoot. "But it might take a machine to get it perfectly right." My sister took off her t-shirt and shorts, her swimsuit solid rose, and tested the temperature of the lake with her toes. The spring sun was pressing screws against my pupils, but the water was perfectly cold, so I eased in, Sarah already swimming the backstroke along the shore, facing the sky with her eyes closed. Our foster mother and father were next, shivering knee-deep in the water, talking about something, their words getting caught in the wind and carried off. After an hour or two, when we'd all had our fill of swimming, we roamed the beach and collected what we could – lung-shaped rocks, broken glass, underwater weeds – and when the sun went cold we gathered back together and loaded up the truck. My sister said she was so hungry she could eat her own arm, so we stopped at a diner on the way home and ate, too beautifully tired to even speak.

There were already airplanes in the sky above Lake Michigan, my sister and I watching them from the L. A fighter jet with wings painted like the American flag screamed above us and dove vertically, nose first, tail spinning towards the water. A boy on the train asked his mother if any were going to crash. "Sometimes they do, but hopefully not today," the mother said. We got off the L and followed the crowd through a heavy heat to the lake, where we laid in the grass near the shore, my sister putting her feet in my lap and telling me to crack her toes, but I pushed them away. Blue Angels flew in formation what seemed like feet above the lake, the blast from their engines leaving waves across the water, the crowd cheering and clapping. "I know what you're thinking, but you can't blame me if it happens. I just need to be ready for anything," my sister said, staring at me for a long time, waiting for me to say something back, say that I understood, but I stayed silent, so she grabbed her backpack and started walking toward the train. I stayed there for another hour after, laying on the grass and thinking up tornados, up entire nights, up entire lives. The horizon cut the sun in half and I walked back to the L with some of the airshow crowd, my heels getting stepped on from behind, a girl holding her father's hand in front of me, looking up at him as he waxed lyrical about airplanes, about wingspans, torque. A cop blew a whistle and waved us across the street and I went up the stairs to the L platform, which was crowded, and stood at a railing overlooking the street. On the sidewalk below there was a dark stain shaped like a smashed guitar and a couple pigeons pecked at it.

He wanted to be in water because of the pain, so we drove down to the YMCA, where we changed in the locker room. I watched him undress, his skin and muscle leaving him a skeleton, and he turned away from me when he caught me staring. We came out of the locker room with our towels over our shoulders and my sister was already in the pool, her hair wet and slicked back. She was a mackerel in any liquid body, her feet like a forked tail, like she could swim both oceans. "You two are so slow," she said and spit a bow of water into the air. Our foster father made his way over to the shallow end and eased into the water, wrapping his arms around himself, shivering. The scar on his neck had healed to a purple S curve and he began to swim along the wall, grabbing hold of the ladder, coughing a time or two, turning to us to smile, treading water. My sister ducked underwater and swam along the bottom of the pool, an inch from the tile, and I followed behind her, feeling the force of her kicking feet. We splashed up right next to him. "I feel weightless. It's good," he said. He paddling with his head just above the surface, from one end of the pool to the other, slowly, like the water was molasses, until he had to stop. A woman who'd been watching us from a deckchair eased herself into the shallow end next to him. "Beautiful children," she said.

Our foster father let my sister drive his truck and she stalled twice and hit a curb. She couldn't park either, so they had to switch seats so he could parallel park in front of our building. Above the living room window a beehive hung from the roof gable, and I glanced at our foster father, because he usually took care of insects and vermin, but he didn't say anything about the bees, even though I knew he noticed. My sister unlocked the main door and we trudged up the stairwell, Maggie's door open a crack, voices and music coming from inside, and Sarah tapped me on the shoulder with her long finger and mouthed that I'd dodged a bullet. Inside our apartment, I made a tomato-and-salt sandwich and sat on the couch next to our foster mother as she watched TV. "Don't be afraid about how little he talks now, or how slow he moves," she said, changing the channel. "He does actually feel better." We watched a show about liquid strings and our foster father came out of the bedroom, already in his sweatpants, kissed our foster mother on the cheek, and sat in his chair next to the TV, his arms and legs looking like they belonged to a recently returned astronaut. The window in the living room was cracked open and wind swirled the curtains and I listened to the bees outside while our foster mother changed channels. And us together like that one last time.

Our foster father lay in the hospital bed with the sheet pulled up to his chin. He looked like a god with his eyes closed. Our foster mother sat next to him, on the edge of the bed, transfixed to the window. The hospital was downtown and the skyscrapers seemed on fire, smoking in the sunrise fog, the wind swirling the low, red clouds. My sister, in a chair right next to him, rubbed his arm over the sheet. And I was near the door listening for the machine to go, and soon it went, and our foster mother rose to her feet, stood over him, grabbed his hand, and said, "It's okay. You can go. We'll be okay, honey. You can go." Her words and the sound of the machine made me drop to my knees, made the sea suck inward, but my sister immediately came over and pulled me off the ground. Together we went over to his bed, my sister right next to me, step for step, and for some reason I reached down and touched his face. I'm not sure why I reached down and touched his face.

Sarah drove our foster father's truck home from the hospital and parallel parked in front of our building on her first attempt. We sat there in silence, the three of us, our foster mother staring out the windshield, probably at other worlds, some world where there was no death because nothing had been born, a barren world, or maybe a world where her husband was still upstairs in the apartment, waiting for us to get home, his tape recorder on his leg, still telling his story, or a world where she'd married someone else and was able to have her own children. It was overcast, but the inside of the truck was humid, and we baked in each other's heat, the neighborhood an event horizon, some kind of dark compression, and we just kept sitting there, trying to learn how to use our eyes again, trying to get it normal, trying to imagine what we faced upstairs, his absence, until finally our foster mother opened the passenger door.

We made our foster mother a sandwich with the lunchmeat he'd bought a few days earlier. My sister grabbed the radio from the kitchen counter and I grabbed the plate and we went down the hallway to the bedroom, where she was in bed, curled in the blankets, her head under her pillow. The windows were closed and the room was dark and smelled like salt and sweat and still him, his clothes, hair, skin, his left behind something, maybe. My sister set the radio on the dresser and began cycling through stations while I sat on the bed with the sandwich plate. The hospital was still in our heads. "Please, Sarah, pick a station," our foster mother said, her voice muffled under the pillow. My sister moved the dial slowly through jazz and rock and religion, turning the volume down a couple notches. It was all old news anyway. Our foster mother eventually rustled out from under her cocoon and sat up in bed, resting her neck against the headboard, gathering her bearings, her shoulders almost all bone, her eyes sunken and her nose purpled from crying. I handed her the plate and she set it on the side table without taking a bite. And for a long time, in the quiet, her body rigid and still, she watched for any sign of movement, for a quarter on the dresser to slide a centimeter, for the blankets to depress with the weight of something, and she listened for any sound, any whisper of him, for his voice to travel back to her somehow, for the radio to change stations on its own, for it to catch his life in its electricity, for his voice to come through its static, fractured or whole, but there was nothing.

After dinner, while we were playing cards at the kitchen table, eating a few figs before we went to bed, the phone rang. Our foster mother got up to answer, yawning into the palm of her hand, and after some initial pleasantries, her voice sank a couple octaves to a growl. She slammed the cordless down on the table and went to her bedroom and came back with her tennis shoes, picking up the phone again to call a cab. Her eyes narrowed like a predator as she spoke, me shuffling the cards into short piles on the tabletop, waiting for her to relay the situation, and after she hung up, she said she was going to the police station. I could feel a bloodletting. The cab honked downstairs and she told me to get some work done and left. I went to my bedroom to work on a few equations and some Renaissance history and then laid back and listened to the end of a Cubs night game on the radio, the bullpen blowing it again. I was half-asleep when they tried to sneak into the apartment, both of them being bat-like, so I gave it a few minutes and then shuffled down to my sister's room. Her bedside lamp was aglow and there was a deep fabric cigarette smell in there, a chain-smoking smell, and she was laughing this quiet, almost arkham laugh, her breath all chemicals. "That house, that White House thing, you should do it. You'd be a hero. You can't just wait for the world to come to you, James," she said, her syllables hanging in her throat an extra second.

Our foster mother was carrying around her screwdriver again and Sarah was packing her backpack. This was all before breakfast, the whole place a booted peace. Our foster mother, her thoughts exhausted, took up the phone and dialed so hard the buttons crunched on the cordless, and Sarah came running out of her bedroom, her socks sliding on the hardwood, and tried to rip the phone away, but our foster mother had too strong a grip. My sister kicked the cupboard under the sink, threw a plate down the hallway, where it shattered into a crescent moon, lifted a kitchen chair and slammed it down. Our foster mother ignored it all, keeping the phone to her ear, to Social Services, or the State, or the police. And Sarah, standing there in the space between words, slowed her breaths and cycled through the different things she could possibly say and the different ways she could possibly say them, and finally whispered something to our foster mother, something careful, and our foster mother whispered something back and hung up the phone and they went to my sister's bedroom to talk.

The living room was a dried worm that Sunday. The TV was off and I wanted it back on. I needed the prosthetic voices, the manufactured sets, the fake ranches, the battlefields. Our foster mother was pacing around the room, pretending to clean, screaming under her breath, and my sister was sitting in our foster father's chair, her eyes dark circles and her hair oily. "I'll get it all back," Sarah said, pleading with our foster mother, and, in some kind of malformed offering, Sarah pulled a necklace from her pocket, a necklace I recognized as our foster mother's, and held it outstretched for her to take back, but it didn't help. Instead, our foster mother ripped open the curtain and stood at the window with her back to us, the sun feasting outside, one of those city afternoons where the heat absorbs straight into the asphalt until it becomes a chemical gum. "Keep the money, Sarah. I don't know what to do, but I know I can't stop you," our foster mother said, her hands nearly blisters from the worrying, from the frantic scrubbing of dishes and screw driving of various appliances. "There's nothing for me here anymore, I guess," my sister said. She went to her bedroom and slammed the door, and our foster mother went to her bedroom too, leaving her door open a crack, as an olive branch. I watched TV, listening to my sister bang around in her bedroom, and ten minutes later she was standing in front of the TV with her backpack over her shoulder. She took a step towards me but I didn't move from my place on the couch, didn't even look up at her. And that was it. I just sat there and watched TV, wanting to be that fiction.

In an alley, next to a dumpster, I tore at my thumbnail, trying to twist it off so a new one would grow. The alley divided two popular bars and there was always something going on, some guy with cracked lips and corner mouth sores trying to hold himself up by his forehead while he pissed against the brick, or some man in a houndstooth jacket smoking a cigarillo like a sparkplug while he went through his wallet, or a businessman rolling his neck and spitting on the ground. My thumbnail was loosening when a large Cadillac pulled up, a woman in a blue dress swinging out from the driver's side door and ducking inside the Goat Bar. The Cadillac was empty and idling, with music coming from inside, and I decided to leave my nail alone and steal it. I checked the apartment windows overlooking the alley to make sure I wasn't being watched, but as I approached the car, the woman burst back through the door, her dress more marine than blue, and I just kept walking, naturally urban. I think I was ready to steal anything, though. Steal every bird from the sky. Steal a fresh eyeball to sell for loose change. Steal gravity. Inertia. But, a solid citizen, I went home instead and loitered outside our apartment building, our foster father's truck still parked out front, the keys hidden somewhere in the apartment.

Like a past life residue, I found something under my pillow one morning. It was one of the tapes our foster father had recorded. Afraid it might contain an unshakable shadow, I didn't listen to it right away, but hid the tape in my desk drawer, where it swelled for a few days, until, eventually, after I couldn't take it anymore, I grabbed the tape recorder from my sister's nightstand. My bedroom door didn't have a lock, so I sat with my back against the woodwork and played the tape, and there was dead air at first, only static, and then our foster father's voice came through, thin and tired, a resurrection. "It's about squeezing out the seconds, I think. It's about burning the wick at every end, but slowly burning it, if that makes sense," he said. I listened to the entire tape and then went to find our foster mother, who was in the living room watching TV, a bland Saturday of simple talk, and when I asked her if she'd put the tape under my pillow, if it was a hint, she said she hadn't, that she'd passed out early, before the sun even went down, so for the few weeks I slept with a couple extra pillows on my bed as an invitation.

Every morning for almost a year I knocked on my sister's bedroom door, hoping for a red cent miracle, but she was never there. Her blankets were how she'd left them, as were the sparse clothes in her closet, and the photos in her nightstand drawer. "I should be home by dinner. Wish me luck," our foster mother called from the bathroom. She was interviewing for jobs all over the city, mumbling old chestnuts in front of the mirror as she got dressed, like, "It is what it is." But it was almost midnight, and she wasn't home, so I wandered around the empty apartment, running my hand along the walls, feeling for divots left by our foster father or for scratches left by my sister. I thought maybe there'd be clues left behind, clues about what I should do next, about where I should go, clues from those already gone. A blue moon shone through the curtains and I stood in the living room and our foster father was back in his chair, healthy again, his face cherub. "It's only darkness, James, but not normal darkness, not your darkness, a beautiful darkness," he said. He was still sitting there when our foster mother got home from wherever she was, her silhouette carved out clean, plainly tired, and he watched her drop to the couch and exhale a tremble, but for some reason he didn't say another word.

The scratch of anything was like a bomb, the apartment an echo chamber, with our foster mother at her new bank teller job, often not getting home until after ten. I listened to Maggie rasp at the walls, mumble in hard spurts, and run the water for a an hour straight, so I went next door and knocked, to see if she could ease the noise, but there wasn't so much as a shuffle behind the peephole. I couldn't listen to her anymore, couldn't listen to myself either, so I went downstairs, unchained my bike from the fence behind our building, and rode around some neighborhoods, the moon only a fingernail fraction above the skyline. There was a city worker up in a cherry picker, a flashlight aimed at a transformer, a guy in a Sox hat carrying a headboard down the street, and someone in a Spiderman costume holding a sign about profiteering outside a donut shop. It must've been the direction of the wind, or some heinous nighttime gravity, but after an hour of riding around I found myself over by the group home again, the corner pretty much the same, except for a dentist's office where the accountant used to be. Even though I'd promised, I'd never been back, my sister telling me that Sammy, Martha, Boom Charlie, and even Sally, the director, had moved on. But just as I was imagining where they all could be – Boom Charlie holed up with anarchists in a factory somewhere, Sammy with the Buddhists, and Sally on an island, in the waves – Martha walked outside and searched the front steps and surrounding sidewalks for cigarette butts. She still looked like an underground heiress, with half her head shaved, and I was about to ride over and reunite but I stopped myself, because, I think, I liked how numb I was becoming.

Our foster mother was cleaning what was already clean, so secretly silver that morning she was almost translucent, an oiled moon. She stopped clawing at the enamel for a second to reach into her pocket and hand me a check. "Before I forget. He wanted to give you more, but the hospital bills," she said. The background of the check was a pattern of blue flowers and I pocketed it without looking at the amount or the memo line, which read, *I love you and happy belated 18th*. "It's enough for a security deposit and a couple months' rent, and if it gets really bad, I have a little more, but only for an emergency, and only a little. But you'll always have a roof over your head no matter what, even if it's with Silvia and me." She went to the kitchen to clean some more, even though the night before I'd packed up the plates, the pots and pans, the glasses, and scrubbed everything down while I listened to news radio, a broadcast about poisoned tap water, our foster mother already hard asleep in her bedroom, with barely a word after she got home from work, her eyes dead-dark tired and the armpits of her blouse sweated through when she trudged through the door.

I only had three boxes of possessions, two of my own and one of my sister's, and I carried them upstairs to my first apartment. I'd helped our foster mother move to Silvia's the day before, but it wasn't much work, because she'd also hired movers, three kids and their father, and she didn't take much with her. She had the movers leave most everything out on the curb, asking me if I wanted the couch or his chair, but I said I wanted to slowly collect my own stuff, that it might be too much. One of the movers was going through my sister's room, which barely held any of her anymore, when he found a shoebox full of cassette tapes in her closet, our foster father's recordings. Our foster mother said she didn't want them, couldn't bear them. "Maybe try to make sense of them," she said. I told her I couldn't bear them either, but she insisted, saying the tapes weren't something to throw away. The place was almost empty, the movers gone, but the scuffs on the hardwood and the divots in the walls were still there, and maybe he was still there, too. Before we locked the door for good, I went into my sister's room, the pinholes from her posters still in the walls, and with the key to my new apartment I etched, Sarah and James were fostered here, into her closet door.

A centipede crawled along the wall, right above my TV, which was on mute, on the news. There was a nagging war, another nosedive scandal, with a story of plastic triumph coming after the commercial break. The apartment was humid, and I decided I wasn't going to kill anything that day, so I just let the centipede crawl, even if it eventually crawled into my ear as I slept. I checked my eyes in the mirror, loneliness a spark, a baseless violence, grabbed my keys from the kitchen counter, and went downstairs, the neighborhood feeling blowhole stuck, and when I finally made it to Montrose station I took the L downtown and walked a few blocks to the museum, which was always free on Tuesdays. It was marbled and clean and cold and almost empty, the air-conditioning humming from the vents above. One painting was an ancient city with its fur burning, another was a fresh peasant dance, another an explicit heaven. I sat on a bench in the middle of a tomb-like room, right underneath the air-conditioning, and watched a girl study the paintings. She had toothpick arms and legs and socks with cartoon cats on them and she stopped at one of the paintings in particular, a blue-shawl portrait of an upper-crust woman in a small, white bedroom, and I swear I heard the girl whisper to herself, "We're all just museums," but when I asked her what she'd just said, her mother quickly appeared and ushered her into the next room, her hand on the small of the child's back, pushing her along, like I was something deranged.

You were gunpowder and you were water and sometimes I still walk the group home, walk its hallways with that seabird smell and go down to the dining room where you eat alone at one of the tables. You look like you've been lucky, like you're in a good place, but when I try to speak to you I always wake, a hooked worm, and turn on the lamp to search under my pillow, in the dresser, in the drawers, but the only thing you left me was this. I need to put on my shoes and wander, and on the street I don't hear sirens or speech, don't see neon or brick. I see only you. I see only you, and time recoils and I think about where you might be. Maybe there are some soft animals outside and maybe there's a different shaped train and maybe you've gone churches or maybe you're junkyards or maybe you're needles or maybe you're music or maybe you're machines or maybe you're here with me and I just can't see it.

Our foster mother would call every Friday to see how work was going, if I was holding up to her recommendation, and to make sure I was still alive, but slowly those calls became every couple of weeks and then every couple of months. I saved small portions of my paycheck and finally bought a bed, instead of sleeping on a mattress on the floor. The living room was still bare, though, except for a TV and wooden stool I found in an alley, and sometimes I wished I'd taken the couch and his chair. I'd been coming home right after work to save money, and one evening when I got home the mailbox was flooded thick with envelopes, so I took the mail upstairs and there was a peculiar letter. The address was handwritten, the letters thin and chopped, like when my sister wrote with her left hand. The return address was fake and there was no name of sender and when I opened the envelope there was a generic grocery store card inside that read, "We hope you're taking off," with a picture of a helicopter. There was no message, no signature, nothing personal, but later that week, the night already a dislocated triumph, with a man breaking beer bottles on the L, I got home from work and made pasta with olive oil and sat on my new bed and read the card again, touching it carefully to feel out the situation.

I wanted to pull as much from the final days of fall as I could. The winter, I could tell, was going to be a months-long harness, the streets already ghost towns after midnight, the late-night wind like liquid nitrogen, freezing your face and opening little stinging cuts inside your nostrils, but the October mornings were tranquil and as I chilled outside, tilting my face upwards to the rising sun, across the street, on the top branch of a skinny, leafless tree, a bird plucked at its feathers like they were the wrong color, like it wanted to shed them and transform. On the curb in front of the tree, below the bird, a woman was sitting inside a parked car, looking at herself in the rearview mirror while she talked on her cellphone. She poked around her bottom lip, adjusted the mirror, turned sideways to see her profile, dropped the phone on the passenger seat, tugged her hair back tightly to her scalp, and then went back to messing with her lip. My inguinal lymph node felt swollen, and I was worried, another past residue, and as I watched the woman in the car mess with her lip I pressed down on the node, under my jeans, until I was sure everything was just my imagination.

Six in the morning and the L shook my apartment. I pulled the blanket over my head and listened to metal squeal only feet from my window. That sound loosened my teeth and ate my tongue most mornings, but that morning, after the train had passed, and before the next one arrived, everything went quiet and I could hear the toddler in the apartment below and I could hear what his mother said to him. The mother, who had this wonderful red hair, and the toddler, who had the same hair, shared what sounded like cereal and a giggle. My spine began to stretch to something like euphoria and I pulled myself out of bed and stood there for a moment to look at my reflection in the darkened window. I looked so malnourished, a sick animal, so I had to look beyond that, and outside to the street, where it was still snowing, where piles of wood and construction equipment were iced over and a man with a scarf wrapped around his face dug out his car with a shovel. Another train was not far off, so I got down on the cold bedroom floor and did twenty pushups, breathing in bursts, trying to gather my thoughts, but like clockwork the L came to scatter me again, so I went to the kitchen, which was at the rear of the apartment, away from the train, and drank four cups of cold coffee while I opened and closed the fridge, which was pretty empty.

I ordered Chinese food and tried to finally eat something, but there was this wound in my head, especially when I closed my eyes, an under-the-eyelids wound, a wound with a familiar touch, somehow memorized and synapsis tattooed. My apartment was quiet and clean, stripped down and bare, with my clothes, including my ties, hung neatly in the closet. I dumped enough salt on my fried rice to shrivel myself to bone and went through some e-mails for work on my laptop. There was a wave of advertisements, a logistical question, two complaints from my boss about my numbers, and an invitation to a housewarming party from someone in the office. While I read, in the downstairs apartment, the mother with the wonderful red hair was talking in basic tones to her toddler again, and I wanted to put my ear to the floor and just listen to them forever, wanted to be that mother, or that toddler, but instead I tried to eat, do work, and when my eyes began to close I rolled my arms and legs into my body to fall asleep on the couch.

I grabbed the pole inside the L for balance and I knew. There was something about its slickness, the feel of its metal, the palm of my hand slightly stinging like a microscopic worm had just gnawed a hole into my skin and wiggled its way in. I looked around the train for the last person who'd touched the pole, a pale, sweaty, hallucinating person, someone who looked too weak to stand for too long, someone drooling down their face, fever talking, someone unleashing guttural throbs from deep within their sore throat. And, sure enough, for the next week I was laid up like a morbid medical case, with symptoms I couldn't exactly identify, a novel virus with fangs. The couple times I willed the strength to crawl from my bed to the bathroom I collapsed on the floor and sweated myself to sleep, my rapid-fire dreams the kind that made you question the fabric of the universe, question if you could easily, if you wanted, slide through the silk of our world and enter the land of the dead. I didn't even have the strength to call our foster mother, but even if she wanted to come over and help, to make chicken soup or check me into intensive care, I wouldn't want her near me, because whatever I had just might be the end of the world. But despite my apocalyptic sickness, I still went to work a day later, so I wouldn't lose my job, even though I was probably Mary Mallon contagious.

The bottom of my right lung hurt like wasps. I'd been thinking about dying too much lately. I drank a cup of cold coffee and stood at the window and watched the L pass, the train, filled to the brim with people, on its way downtown, stains of stalwart graffiti on the sides of the last two cars, a fascist rat and a bumpy signature. I finished my coffee and as I dressed for work I thought about the day before, about how I'd sat at my desk most of the morning drawing opaque eyes and zen craters on sheets of computer paper while caffeine pills blasted my brain with chemical sun. A coworker, Mia, came out of the elevator, her face flushed and her bag hanging off her shoulder, and I locked my computer screen and cut her off in the hallway, saying we should take the afternoon off. "Let's bite the bullet," she said, and we took the elevator down to the street and walked around the block a few times. A news van was parked on a corner and a man in a fur hat with a microphone was stopping people on the street to ask them questions. We walked by and he asked us if we had anything to say, anything to contribute to the unfolding story, and we both said we didn't.

Mia from work asked me out, saying both of us were cloistered lepers and that it was time to live a little. She chose the place, an Ethiopian restaurant in Lakeview, and I took the train to meet her, my eyes spinning inside their sockets and my hands a shaking mess. I arrived before her and chose a table in the back, a sand-and-spice smell embedded in the furniture, the scattered pottery. Mia walked in about fifteen minutes later, her hands shaking, too. We hugged and sipped our waters and ordered, and when the food came we ate with our hands and it was carnal. "They only promote the heartless," Mia said. After we finished eating, we split the check and left the restaurant and walked to the train, the city a frozen echo, both of us wearing ski hats and gloves. "Do you think I should come over?" she said, and I said I thought she should, but warned her about my lack of furniture. We took the train to Uptown and walked the few blocks from the station to my apartment, Mia hooking her arm around mine, the feeling of it a brain zap, a withdrawal. "You have to find something to fill this place up. It's like nobody even lives here," she said when she walked into my apartment. We stood in the empty living room and kissed, a nighttime winter wind shaking the window, and she took off her sweater and I kissed her breasts and her neck extended and she undid her jeans, her legs still cold, and sometimes just live a little.

It was a winter romance, and we were at another restaurant, an Indian place, watching the snowfall go velvet through the window. I drank half a glass of water and asked her what she was like as a child. "Do you ever think back at something you did as a kid and shudder at the sheer stupidity? But then you have to remember that you were just young, and you can't hold yourself to the same standards. That's a horror, really. That whole thing. Reconciling the now you with any version of you before," Mia said. She took a couple bites of her biryani and then asked me about mine, so I told her I was essentially an orphan, that it was a story as old as time, that my sister and I grew up in a group home and then moved to a foster home later, that my sister was gone at eighteen, that she must've needed a full-fledged escape, and I wasn't sure where to. "You must have some tough memories to shudder about then. This is how I do it; I tell myself I'm going to remember, one last time, in the greatest possible detail, something I never want to remember again, no matter how tough a memory, and then I can forever delete it. Sometimes it works, but mostly it doesn't. So, if I can ask, and don't answer if you don't want to, but what happened to your mother?" Mia said and I'm still thinking about that question.

Spring came and Mia invited me over to her apartment, which was a low-ceiling studio, for our last meal together. She'd found another bank job in Ohio, her home state. It was a bit more money and she'd be closer to family, to her ailing mother. "She needs me right now, even though sometimes when I needed her, she wasn't there," Mia said. She made a fragile eggplant and we ate on her couch, our plates on the coffee table, her apartment almost as barren as mine, with most everything boxed up. A night like that can last years, when someone leaves before you're able to learn more, say more, know more, and she could sense her leaving was my small death, so she moved closer to me on the couch. "It might be too melancholy, but one last time?" she asked. And it was a cage of spilled paint, an untethered expression inside a formula, and afterwards I asked her what she'd remember most about the city, and she said loneliness packed together.

I took pills. I drank tea and honey. I closed my eyes and invented stories where I was the hero, where I identified and tackled a school shooter before he got off a single shot, where I rearranged our entire currency, where I climbed the White House fence and set myself on fire on the lawn, but sleep was still a dream. In the living room, where I'd left the TV on a low murmur, a late-night movie playing like an old wart, I pushed my ear against the cold floor, hoping to hear the child and his mother that lived below, hoping to hear anything that was halfway pure, but instead I heard something that sounded like a sleeping, starving dog. I read a book about poker until the sun rose and then I dressed and took the L downtown, early for work. A silver SUV almost hit a light post on the corner as I sat on the ledge near the lobby doors of my office building, on the spikes designed to keep the homeless away, and smoked three cigarettes in a row while a pigeon with a blow dart stuck in its wing ate an insect, legs and all, in the middle of the sidewalk.

Work that day was a drowned beetle, the train its decomposition, the walk home from the station its tiny skeleton. Back at my apartment, I called our foster mother because she'd left a message about how she needed the sink in her apartment fixed. She didn't answer, her voicemail full for some reason, so I ironed my shirt for the next day and went through the clothes in my closet, finding some I could give to Goodwill, whittling down what I didn't need. About an hour later she called back and described the problem with her sink, how precious water was being wasted, and I told her I'd be over there tomorrow. She also talked about the new condos going up in her neighborhood, which she said were an eyesore, and contagious. And because she asked, I told her work was fine, that I was taking care of myself, socializing, and, so she wouldn't worry, that I was aiming for a promotion. She told me how last Friday she'd gone down to the lake and walked around by herself until it got dark. She said she planned to go out there at least a couple times a week to watch the sunset, so she could feel like part of the world again herself.

The far west side of Chicago and everyone seemed like they had secret signs of arson, like all their faces had been burned. I'd brought my toolbox and followed our foster mother to the kitchen, where the cabinet below the sink was already cleaned out so I could work. I got down on the floor, stuck my head under the sink, inspected the old pipes, inspected the severity of the leak, the overall rust. Silvia, our foster mother's housemate, whom she'd met at a garage sale when Silvia was selling most of her possessions after her husband's aneurysm death, walked into the kitchen and stood over me, hovering. I had no idea what I was doing so I banged on a pipe with a wrench. "What a good son you have, Elizabeth. Tell us if you need anything," Silvia said. I told them I'd be fine, to keep doing what they were doing. "We were just watching TV. Did you see what the president said yesterday?" our foster mother said. I didn't answer and instead banged on a pipe again and the two of them slowly made their way back to the living room. It took me three hours to halfway fix the sink. Water still leaked when the faucet was on full blast, but I hoped they wouldn't notice. I called for them to come inspect my work and ran the sink just strong enough to the hide the leak, Silvia bending down to check the cabinet for any new wetness, her hair thin and her scalp visible. When they were satisfied we all went to the living room, had a cup of coffee, and watched the news. One side of the living room was clearly our foster mother's, with framed pictures of our foster father and us, her radio, and some books on a small bookshelf, and the other half of the room was Silvia's, her pictures mostly of a lone man, probably her husband, with spools of fabric for her dressmaking laid across the wooden chair of a writing desk and her collection of old records, most of them country, haphazardly piled on the floor.

The walls of my apartment were skin thin, so I'd get a glass from the kitchen and put it against the bedroom wall and listen to my next-door neighbor, a violinist. "I can't keep it. It's too much," he said one summer evening. "Maybe medicate instead," he said one midnight. "I'm sorry but I don't care," he said before work one Friday. One night he came home loud and late and I got the glass and listened to him fuck, trying to remember how it felt, the calm and the storm of it. I coughed hard and they stopped and his voice went to a whisper and I pulled the glass carefully from the wall and stood motionless in my bedroom for five minutes. A few days later, when I was outside talking to the mother with the wonderful red hair about longwinded justice and rising rents, the next-door neighbor came walking up the street with crates stacked full of sheet music, which he dropped with a grunt on the sidewalk. I asked him if he needed help carrying one of the crates upstairs and he said, "If you could. It's been a day." I lugged the crate upstairs and for a moment, while he thanked me, and before he closed the door, I could see inside, and his countertops were devastated with dirty dishes and there were clipped apart magazines flung everywhere and at least a dozen melted medieval candles on his stove.

It was 2:30 in the morning, but I was still awake, reading a book about manifest destiny, my bedroom window cracked open so I could listen for any macabre city noises, for screams of joy or pain or both simultaneous, a single, reverberating, far-off gunshot, for tires screeching before a crash, when my neighbor took up his violin and began to play long bass moans, the calm swell a reminder of Sammy. The instrument got inside my head, and what of this world is a true gift, and when is nothing hidden from us, and show me a soul that isn't only bone. He played for another half hour, and in the morning, when I was sitting on the top step of the back stairwell of the building, drawing slim quasars in a notebook and smoking, he came outside, already dressed to the nines, maybe for a concert, his hair styled like a futuristic gypsy. "Sorry if I was loud last night. I hope you can't hear me when I play," he said. The trash bag he was carrying was see-through and inside there were empty bottles of wine, and I moved aside on the stairwell so he could take the trash downstairs.

His music was wrought with something wild that morning, like he was under a dense canopy in a jungle, his combinations of notes a primal throat song. I still had a headache from the night before, from sitting in a bar by myself, heavily drinking and watching the night unspool, but his music began to loosen the pain and I clanked an empty drinking glass against the bedroom wall, the floorboards creaking like a mother. The violin went quiet, which made me notice my headache again, and I heard the rear door of his apartment open, and then there were a series of strong knocks at my door. I didn't answer, only listened, the sliding metal of a delivery truck in the alley, him talking out on the landing, outside my door, saying something that sounded like, "I'm not your entertainment," and for once in my life, I think, I knew where I stood.

I saw my sister on the far west side, near our foster mother's apartment. It must've been a secret visit. I was on the patio of an aimless restaurant, drinking and watching a man in a tattered jersey collect money, when she appeared like a loud, long death, coming down the sidewalk straight towards me, walking in strong steps, with a spool of fabric tucked under her arm, blue silk, and a diaper bag over her shoulder. A velvet animal, her fingers, her wrists, her neck, her dark eyes were all the same, her legs, the scar on her knee, her curly hair, all the same, and my vision blurred and soon my sight collapsed to rheumy shadows. "Sarah," I said. Oh, with our dying hearts, kids. "Sarah," I said again, and louder, standing from my chair on the patio. It was early afternoon and the street was a diesel menace, with cars burning away every small sound, but she must've felt something, because she stopped and turned. "James," she said, and I made my way towards her. "I just can't, James. I'm sorry," and she turned back and hustled down the street and I waited there in history.

I was a lone thunderstorm for a few years and then I met Mary at a museum downtown. We saw each other from across the room, a charred glass globe hanging from the ceiling in exhibition, Mary with huge eyes and dark hair and me in my hooded sweatshirt. We started to move loosely through the museum, glancing at each other, the security cameras on us like thieves. I stood in front of a painting, a zinc blue apparatus, and she came and stood next to me, her speaking first, a soft comment about the state of my shoes, and I remember I laughed, which is always something. After a few months, a handfuls of dates, some nights together, a half-spilling of our secrets, a couple lies, I moved into her apartment, both of us nearly broke and class stuck, with old newspapers for lungs, and we thought the split rent might help. We ate and shopped and watched TV. We talked about dogs and maybe children. One summer night, we were at an Italian restaurant and Mary was rolling her neck in circles, stretching her spine, her loving comfort above all else. "Everybody always wants something from me. Just try to give me something back," she said.

Mary and I wandered the racks of a three-story department store on the mag mile. She bought some jeans and I bought some shoes and we walked around downtown with our shopping bags, joking about the night before, when neither of us could sleep so we stripped down and went some kind of umbilical. "Whatever that whirling dervish move was, that slow but fast thing, save it, and after we have a fight do it again and I'll forgive you," she said. In front of us on the sidewalk, a group of tourists suddenly stopped to take pictures of the skyline. It was cloudy and the skyscrapers looked like long letters. "If Chicago was a color, what color would it be," one of them said. We hung around downtown for a couple more hours, drank a few beers at a bar, watched an allegorical street performer, ate at a sandwich shop, and shopped again. In the late afternoon we stood on a bridge that overlooked the river and she kissed me.

Mary had her feet up on the coffee table, painting her toenails red, wearing a white sundress, her legs suntanned. It was summer and there was a street festival outside and the speakers were right below our apartment window and the sound of an 80's cover band drowned out the TV, but we watched anyway. We watched a woman split a teacup open, a whale swim holes in the sand, and a slow detective incense burn. Mary told me to change the channel and we watched a judge collect jars of eyes. We watched a girl shake sugar awake with diamonds. We watched commercials. Then we just couldn't watch anymore, so we took the L downtown and walked around until Mary had to take her shoes off. We sat on a bench by the water, the river dark blue beneath the growing shadows of the skyscrapers and asked each other questions we couldn't answer. "What's one thing you would undo?' Mary said, reaching down to rip a hanging piece of skin from the heel of her foot. "And what's the first thing you think about when you wake up?" It was symphonic, the summer nightfall, Chicago in bloom, and when it was dark we went home and she put on the only lingerie she owned and told me what to do and I did it. The bedroom was small, with barely enough room for a dresser, and the nights were hot and claustrophobic, us sticking together under a single sheet. In the morning my lungs hurt and I went out to the kitchen and Mary was sitting at the table with a caterpillar crawling along the back of her hand. She smiled when she saw me, already with a cup of coffee in front of her. The caterpillar looked like an arched spine and she shook it free and it fell to the kitchen table, where it crawled towards a thin line of sunshine on the wood.

Mary was eating a bowl of Neapolitan ice cream on the couch and I was sitting next to her with the hood of my sweatshirt pulled over my head, watching TV. She cupped the bottom of the wide porcelain bowl and brought it to her mouth and slurped. I changed the channel and we watched a shadow man make love. We watched the intestines of a great war. We watched a queen become herself. Mary moved closer to me and put her feet in my lap, asking me to rub her scabbed heel. Like she knew my memories. Our apartment was becoming lived in, becoming our home. We could move around at night without having to turn on the lights, without having to feel along, but when things got too comfortable, Mary would change around the furniture, rearrange the contents of the drawers in the kitchen, hang new curtains. "Each week let's do one new thing. Something neither of us has done before. Less TV. More life," she said. Her eyes were burning a hole in my cheek so I finally turned off the TV to face her and she recommended we go on a diet of only water, cayenne pepper, and lemon.

Our bodies were flying low like bombers, like we wanted to detonate our landscapes, the skyline view from our hotel room window unlocking something in us. It was overcast and downtown was a dark smoke and we were as naked as paper, looking out the eleventh-story window, watching the economics of it all, the totem and time and slurp of the city, and after a few minutes, after we'd brushed our teeth and were physically ready again, on the starched hotel sheets, we got down again, this time with utmost caring, with eye contact, despite the bandage on Mary's forehead, until the final two minutes, when we both really let loose a nasty fever. After, still in bed, we read a brochure about the history of the hotel, about how three previous presidents had stayed there. Mary ripped the brochure from my hand and threw it across the room and got up to run a hot bath, telling me how free she felt, despite what had happened the day before, when she'd rose from the couch and suddenly fainted. Her eyes had rolled to the back of her head and she'd dropped right there in the living room, banging her head on the coffee table, and I'd stood there, looking down at her, wondering what to do. Her eyes slowly opened and when she saw my worried face she started laughing, some sick cackle. I helped her to the couch and went to get a towel for her head and when I came back from the kitchen she said she felt fine. "We're still definitely taking our domestic hotel vacation downtown tomorrow," she said. Blood dripped from her eyebrow and ran down her nose and as I put the towel to her head I could see how deep the wound really was.

We were radiating monogamy. Mary had a glob of mustard on her chin and her bratwurst was long gone. She downed the rest of her beer from a clear plastic cup, staring up at the sun between sips, wearing her big black sunglasses. We wandered a street festival in an unfamiliar neighborhood where full-sized flags hung from balcony banisters. There were food tents on both sides of the closed-off street, lining the sidewalks like a corral, and we drifted down the centerline with the crowd. Mary finished another beer and pulled me inside a corner boutique to see if they had anything interesting. It was an eclectic death in there and she went straight to a display of rings near the cash register. "This one has cloudy forest power," she said, and I bought her the ring with my credit card and signed the slip without looking at the price. After we shared a big pretzel on a bench in front of a record store, we left the street festival and walked back to our apartment, slipping down as many side streets as possible so we could walk in peace, the wind drying the sweat on our foreheads. We turned a corner and Mary suddenly shrieked and made a beeline toward a tiny dog on the sidewalk. It was an old animal, with stubby, twisted front legs and labored breathing, and Mary petted behind the dog's ears, the owner with the leash annoyed. "If we got a dog it would probably die in like two days," she said. The clouds were dragon-backed and disappearing into evening, and when we finally made it to back to our apartment, Mary put the turquoise ring on her left hand just to see.

The air was ingrown with sirens and police were stuck to their radios, almost omniscient on the humid streets, the sound of their coded static around every corner, Chicago submerged in hot weather, summer violence. I was standing outside a near north side dive bar, smoking, pondering Mary dynamics, the building across the street, a health clinic, humming with people. The door of the bar swung open and music filtered out and a woman came outside and leaned against the brick. She was wearing a ripped t-shirt and jeans, her bangs stuck to her forehead with sweat, looking like the opposite of an early, random death, like she could dodge the bullets out there. She lit a cigarette and two men from the bar busted outside in laughter, one of them wearing a gigantic silver watch and the other digging inside his pockets for what was probably money. "Let's hedge our bets and hit up the club," one of the men said. The woman looked at me with wry rebellion and I lit another, and as we smoked we glanced at each other a few times, the sound of an ambulance a few blocks west, something crawling in me, something desperate, or maybe something hopeful, or probably just something I thought was halfway new.

We didn't get to Milwaukee until after midnight, the motel rundown and soiled, but we still jumped right to the nasty, going as native as allowed, all tongues, sticky and sheen, Mary talking about her sensations, what it felt like, more than she usually did. In the morning, before the music festival, we ate breakfast at a local diner, the window greased with fingerprints, the good land a war chest for wolves. "Everything here smells like yeast. It's in my hair," Mary said, and she ordered pancakes and I ordered waffles and it was bliss to be out of Chicago, bliss to know I was only a visitor, a mysterious stranger, like I could use any name I wanted. The waitress ducked behind the lunch counter to change her apron, her previous one noticeably soaked with some morbid liquid, when a family of three walked in, a girl about four years old, with hearing aids, riding on her father's shoulders. And maybe it was the fourth cup of coffee, or it was that family, or probably it was Mary, who was cryptic energy that morning, her eyes oak saturated, wearing her white tank top and black bra and dark jeans, the combination of which was carnal magic, but I leaned across the table and asked her if she would marry me, eventually, that if I were to ask, in the future, would she? "I wouldn't be wasting my time otherwise. I'm not only in this for the pleasure," she said.

Mary was spraying an entire bottle of spider killer around the foundation of our apartment, an old Chicago duplex. The owners, an elderly couple, still lived in the apartment below and the husband came outside to see what Mary was spraying. She stopped to talk to him and with the second-floor window cracked open I could hear them from my spot on the couch, the chemical smell drifting upstairs into the living room. "They come crawling in during winter. Need to hit them in the fall," I think I heard Mary say. I got up from the couch and snuck a peek down at them, the husband in his Sunday best and Mary with her hair under a red bandanna. They talked a while longer and then the husband went back inside and Mary started spraying again. After she'd exhausted the bottle, she came upstairs and we cooked something together for dinner, Mary preparing the chicken and me chopping the vegetables, and when it was finished, we sat across from each other at the table and judged our meal, concluding we were thumbless chefs. She grabbed a Jamaican beer and went to the living room to watch her Sunday night show about slow revenge and I did the dishes, a spider crawling across the wall above the sink. I thought about telling her, but kept it quiet.

I found the west coast playoff game on the radio, the Rockies versus Diamondbacks, and listened to the entire thing in the living room in the dark so Mary wouldn't wake, the Rockies winning well past midnight with a late-inning double. My brain still busting through sleep, I got out the tape recorder and went through some of his tapes until I found what I wanted. Our foster father coughed a couple times before speaking. "We could see the swamp from where we were up in this tree, dragonflies and mosquitoes, big buzzard ones, flying around the water, and sure enough my cousin pointed to an alligator out there sunning itself in the mud. My cousin, a born and raised panhandle kid, wanted to go down and get closer to the gator, but I sure as hell didn't. I wanted to stay up in the tree, where it or anything else that hung around that swamp couldn't touch me. I don't remember what he said to convince me, but we ended up climbing down and sneaking through the reeds, which tore up my legs something horrible, and when we finally got through to the swamp we were right on the backside of this gator. We stopped in our tracks, staying completely still, my cousin going for the big rock next to his feet, bending down slowly to, I knew, throw at the gator, but then the thing stretched out its body, raised its neck, seeming to get even bigger, and my cousin dropped the rock and we ran like hell all the way back his dad's place."

The first snowfall of the season and I was ready for the city to stomach me, for it to digest my body away. Mary was next to me, folding her clothes and arranging them in neat piles on the floor, a basket of clean laundry at her feet. She really did have the biggest eyes, like onyx globes, like they contained every image ever witnessed by a human. "If I had to, I'd bet fifty on the horsemen, if Revelations happened," she said, balling up her final pair of washed socks and throwing them into the basket. "The end will be bad and I'd put my money on violence." On TV a preacher staged a show for the congregation, my blood an orchestra, way too caffeinated for the late evening, so I told Mary I'd be right back, that I was going to run up to the store, if she wanted anything, and she said chocolate coffee. The street was a littered glacial sheet and I pushed through the wind, the hood of my jacket pulled over my head, snow blowing in my face, and as I passed the tavern on the corner, I looked through its thin window and inside there were men in top hats and women in long wool dresses. Some of them danced old dances on the scuffed pine floor, some drank large glasses of dark beer at the brass bar, some played billiards, lining up shots with cigarettes dangling from their mouths, a couple kissed in the corner shadows, and I stood there in the falling snow, looking through that window, knowing they were probably all ghosts, long dead, most of them buried in Graceland cemetery, all of them on borrowed city time.

Mary and I were at a bar downtown, drinking like trees. "You're a liar. The first settlers didn't eat people as part of their normal cuisine," she said, leaning back in her chair and stretching her neck toward the ceiling, a drop of gin or tonic above her lip. The music sounded like a cracked windshield and she grabbed the back of my neck and squeezed it. "Unlike today's world, if they did eat people, it was out of necessity," she said. She paid the tab and we left the bar and on the cab ride home I could feel her heartbeat inside my chest somehow, the city speeding by, frozen leather and teeth. She opened her purse, took out her phone, and tried to call somebody again, somebody who never answered. I asked her about it and she said, "Hey, I've got a great idea. Why don't you go ahead and tell me about your sister some more? Or Sammy? That's always fun." Her breath was a tourniquet and the bars were all closing and people were sliding around on the iced streets and we were stuck in frozen mix traffic, the alcohol becoming more pronounced. When we finally got home, Mary kicked off her boots at the top of the stairs and went right to the bedroom while I sat on the couch in the dark, the streetlights only enough to see the outline of our furniture, and her phone rang in the bedroom, and I heard her laugh, so I turned on the TV and watched a silver-clad woman turn blue. I must've passed out, and when I woke Mary was standing over me, balancing both feet on the armrest of the couch, her ear against the wall. "Do you fucking hear that?" she said. "It's rats. It sounds like rats." There was definitely something inside our walls, an animal, scratching around, and we sat there and listened for a long time, flashes from the TV lighting up her eyes. "I'll be sorry for this, I guess. Sometimes I think I know what I want, but I can fall in love with anyone," she said, and the scratching in the wall went quiet for a moment and her phone rang in our bedroom.

A pill bottle rattled and Mary called for me from the bedroom and when I went in there she was hunched over the nightstand with a hollowed-out pen to her nose, snorting. She handed me the pen and crushed another pill to dust. "What do you want to do today?" she said. The doctor across the street from our apartment, a doctor with the whitest shirts I'd ever seen, who sometimes smoked cigarettes around the corner, who a month earlier had asked me if I was having trouble focusing, who'd pushed the question about medication again on the next visit, had now helped Mary with her focus. "Maybe the skin of everyone is the same. Like maybe everyone on earth is one giant skin chopped into people shape, like we're just one part of the same huge outer layer," she said. I snorted the pill in eight slow clumps because the inside of my nose was twisted and I couldn't get enough suction. In bed, we had our heads where our feet were supposed to be, thumping like malfunctioning robotics, Mary's hands always familiar, like she was a reincarnation, and that was the hardest part, the thought of some new set of hands.

I thought I'd found Sarah, even though she had a different last name. I called from my work phone, her possible banking information on the screen right in front of me, a meager checking account, no savings account, and a credit card. As the phone rang, I went through the transaction history of the checking account: automatic payments to a TV service, a coffee shop every day, but often not the same shop, or even a shop in the same town, a grocery store transaction around $70 pretty much every week, save for a week when she was using her debit card in Arizona, probably on vacation, most of the purchases there for restaurants and liquor stores, a monthly ACH withdraw for what looked like healthcare, and a bi-monthly direct deposit from a law office, her paycheck. The phone kept ringing and I dove into my desk drawer for an old pack of cigarettes and, after my third attempt calling, when nobody answered, I locked my computer screen and went downstairs to smoke. Lake Street had been closed off since morning and a service crew in orange vests were messing around near an open manhole. It was a dead gray day downtown, with hanging faces in bus windows, and I finished my cigarette, put the butt in the blue dispenser near the front doors, and looked one last time at the service crew before I went back inside, hoping like a zealot that one of them would saw through a fiberglass cable or short circuit a fuse box and plunge us into a forever blackout.

Someone at work stuck a note to my computer screen while I was in the bathroom, in front of the mirror, studying my bloodshot eyes, unsure about how human I was. The note read, *my office pronto*, and I knew what it was all about. My boss's office was a migrant universe, with three steaming Tupperware containers on his desk, the smell of charred meat, cool ranch, and celery salt colliding. He wasn't eating, though. He was standing at the window, the sounds of busses and cabs rising from the street, a curbside argument, a police whistle. He turned around and smiled, pretending he was loose and free, but he was too confined to be anything other, with his pressed gray suit and gel-parted hair. "You've been short credit cards three months in a row. Do you like working here? Be honest," he said. He had a small spit bubble of ranch in the cleft of his chin, and I didn't say much back, only that my accounts would come around, that I had an action plan for achievement. He gave me a notebook with the logo of the bank on the cover and I left his office and walked down the hallway and back to the bathroom. The janitor was mopping up something venomous in the back stall and he watched me stare at my eyes in the mirror and he heard how I talked to myself. I left the bathroom, poking at my eye, pretending my contact was messed up, making a small production out of it so everybody would think they knew why I was always in there.

Mary was in the northern suburbs visiting her mother, so I had the place to myself. I was outside, on the small balcony of our apartment, shivering and smoking as many cigarettes as I could, our next-door neighbor, the manager of a supermarket deli, washing dishes in his kitchen window. I imagined someone, as an act of possibly ill-conceived grassroots war, going to his supermarket with syringes full of something heinous and injecting the fruit and vegetables, leaving small punctures in the tangerines and avocados. The cops might catch the person, or they might not, but probably not in time to track down all the customers who'd purchased the injected produce. Or maybe, in another scenario, this person would hide in the supermarket bathroom on the off chance they weren't cleaned before the store closed, and when everybody had left, the person would go to the BBQ aisle, grab all the lighter fluid, and douse the place. I lit another cigarette and the neighbor looked over and saw me watching him in his window and he closed the blinds, his eyes still in the gaps between for another five minutes.

Mary stole the TV remote and hid it somewhere in her bedroom. We were sleeping separately now, like the diseased, her in the bedroom, on a made bed, with pills, and me, on an air mattress in the living room, with alcohol. "I'll be home, I think," she said and left for work, the elementary school. I searched like she would hide, trying to capture her mindset, her way of thinking, to find the spots she thought were most secret – inside her pillowcase, behind a false wall panel, taped to the inside of her lampshade. In the back of her closet, shoes were stacked shin high and on the shelf, behind a plastic bin, there was a duffel bag zipped tight, with dozens of photos inside, mostly of her father, who'd had a stroke when she was teenager. I thought about the heredity of it all, and how Mary would lose her footing often, her balance, and sometimes even tumble completely, losing consciousness, like when she'd hit her head on the coffee table, but her future was becoming less of a concern, so I just kept looking for the remote, opening her dresser drawers and running my hand underneath her folded clothes, careful to remain a ghost, finding, in the bottom drawer, an unknown-to-me, opened box of condoms with a couple missing. I finally found the remote under her bed, in a shoebox, wrapped in a hippie bandana, and I unwrapped the bandana and displayed it in full view, open and obvious for her on the coffee table, and then went to work myself.

Mary dipped her hair back into the bathwater. I could feel her slipping away in small amounts, in light touches and singular words, in grace and anger; the day before, I'd heard her crying in the stairwell after work, but when she finally came inside she was all smiles, despite her eyes, and earlier in the week, in the middle of the night, I'd caught her sneaking out to the living room and standing over my air mattress as I pretended to sleep. She'd wanted to say something, to do something, maybe, but she just stood there motionless and I didn't move an inch either. "I don't think I'm built for this place. Sometimes I just want it over," I told her. And the moment those words left my lips, Mary's face became a fever and she lunged for me, a pure predator, unleashing her spine and unhinging her joints, stretching out her fingers to claws, water dripping off her shoulders and down the front of her, the bathtub overflowing, and she grabbed my hair and palmed my face and slammed my head back against the faucet, pinning me back against the ceramic, her fingernails dug into my shoulders and her lips pressed against my ear so hard it hurt. "Nobody was built for this place, asshole," she said. Her heartbeat was stark, her chest pumping, arteries expanding, and she climbed on top of me and wrapped her arms around my neck tighter than she ever had before. "Just close your eyes and listen, just listen, James," she said. And the bathroom window cracked from the outside cold and the drone of the TV in the other room, and listen, are you listening, and the juice of an eye blinking, the grind of molars, a slide of jointed bone, a pluck of water, and I opened my eyes and Mary. Thank you.

I was taking a shower and Mary came into the bathroom like she often did when I didn't lock the door. I peeked around the shower curtain and noticed a suitcase and canvas bag full of presents in the hallway. "I'm going to my mom's for Christmas. I'm probably not coming back until you're gone," she said. Her eyes half water, her hands full fists, she stood there waiting for me to unfold a perfect sentence and save us, but I stayed silent, waiting for her to speak instead, for her to reveal the blackholes in our relationship, like she'd done so many times before, to explain how we could work to collapse them, to recommend actions, to maybe simply love each other again, but she didn't say a damned word either, just walked out of the bathroom, leaving the door open, and I pressed my forehead against the tiles, let the hot water carve away at me, the steam escaping the bathroom to flood the apartment, the fire alarm going off in the hallway, me jumping out of the shower to rip the blasted thing right off the wall.

I stared at the TV and tried to remember how exactly it worked, its insides, its lenses, but I doubted I was right. The show was about how society flakes away until only loose change spins. It came on every Tuesday night at nine. In that episode, the acting president called in a herd of helicopters and commanded them to slide low over a city and stalemate all the people with sound. A piano solo played during the end credits and I fell asleep on the couch with the hood of my sweatshirt over my head, my new apartment a disassembled clock. A rainstorm pummeled the window and I think I saw her in a dream. She asked me if I still loved her and I told her I've loved everybody I've ever met, how sometimes it's as simple as the way you hum low like wasps when you read, or touch your fingers to a table, or it's the blue veins just under the skin of your wrists, or it's how you close your eyes when it all becomes too much, how you run your hand along your neck and smile, how you are music no matter, your beautiful disasters, your graceful shames, or it's the violins of these nights out here, all of us, together, the slow peel of everything we once were, how we're still here, the chance, choice, fate, birth and death of it, and sometimes we want something more, or sometimes we don't want anything at all, and sometimes we forget love, sometimes we forget how the slow move a hand, the soft move of a mouth, our bodies, can breathe life into each other. And I love you if I've ever met you. But I'm going back to sleep.

I sat on the edge of my bed and called Carly, getting the $220 together, the back pages. She called back a few minutes later, her phone cutting in and out, a hum of something digital in the background. She told me about an hour, so I got myself together in the bathroom, the ceiling sagging toward the corners. I tried to patiently wait, but it was impossible, so I scrubbed the enamel from the dishes, cleaned the black stains on the top of the fridge, peeled the haunted strips of wallpaper from the kitchen walls. Carly came up the stairs about two hours later and I opened the door before she could knock and we went to the bedroom and her hands were calloused and she was all chemical perfume, jet fuel, and she'd brought her own condoms. I grazed the mole on her left hip and her hair smelled like cinnamon alcohol and she began to breathe heavier, her spine outstretching, some initials tattooed on her shoulder blade. She moved her hips until a heatwave and I was all wax. "Excuse me, hon," she said and went to the bathroom for hygiene and came back to ask me if I could do two, if I wanted two, everything now a new kind of frigid, and I searched the floor for my jeans and found my wallet. Her knees cracked when they hit the mattress again and I put my hands on her waist and together we breathed and breathed and then our time was up.

The ceiling of my bathroom had caved in overnight from the weight of the snow, with a hole above the toilet large enough for a raccoon to crawl through. Snowflakes drifted down and dissolved on the circus-stained linoleum floor, so I shut the bathroom door as tightly as I could, to forget, poured another cup of cold coffee, and went to the front window. It was still early, and every footprint in the snow was deep and new, the trees bladed icicles, two women talking in the entryway of the building across the street. One of the women had a hard cast on her right foot and I imagined what had happened. How she'd probably hammered away at herself one lonely night, with her foot perched on the kitchen table and a washcloth between her teeth for the pain. She'd closed her eyes and raised the hammer and smashed at her toes because she'd realized that she'd sacrificed her entire life, her entire self, every desire, every dream for her children, and now her children were pillaging this place dry.

We all hammered along on a Tuesday. The office smelled like industrial carpet cleaner and baby wipes and the heat was cranked up too high. I couldn't sell anything, most potential customers hanging up before I could even finish a sentence, except one woman who mistook me for her dog groomer. I locked my computer per procedure, for the safety of customer information, opened the bottom drawer of my desk, took a caffeine pill, a bee, without so much as a gulp of water, and then walked around the office, trying to start a conversation, any conversation. Michael, who I sometimes got a beer with after work, looked up from his computer, his face a blotchy mahogany. "Did you see this e-mail about serious repercussions if we don't hit loans? They do that shit just to keep us in lockstep," he said. His eyes were sunken and bloodshot and I could tell he was still hurting raw. Last month, he'd taken time off work because he'd lost his son to a stillborn birth, his wife becoming a private cloud, he said, that she was simply drifting detached, that he was worried, that she was taking way too many vitamins, almost overdosing on nutrients, because she thought she'd failed her body, and this failure was the reason for her child's death. "Time for a round or three, I'd say," Michael said, printing the e-mail about the loans for his paper trail, but I told him I was going to the Humane Society after work to adopt a dog, the direst stray there, the one with holes and scars, so we'd have to grab a beer another time.

The dog I adopted from the Humane Society was Machiavellian. She loved things being afraid of her, loved to bark, her bark a monster for her size, at only fifty pounds. At the pet store, I bought her a crate, collar, leash, some chicken and sweet potato dog food, and a squeak toy in the shape of a stingray, which she destroyed immediately, scattering its insides around my apartment. The first day home she mostly roamed, incessantly sniffing at something under the fridge, probably something terribly dead or dying, barking at the smallest noise in the stairwell, even the wind, and scratching at the front door. I took her for a long walk around the neighborhood and people crossed the street when they saw the scars on her nose, the muscles of her legs, and by Sunday night she was asleep next to me on the bed, her large, pointed ears not twitching to every noise, seemingly content. But in the morning, a hard slap from my water state, I woke to her barking like a hunted wolf, and when I went out to the living room, she was under the coffee table, growling and showing her teeth, her eyes on my every move, my every tick. I called in sick to work, fed her, and we went for another long walk, her tongue hanging out like a feeler, and just when she seemed like she was calming down, was losing some fear, a bus suddenly pulled up to the curb next to us with its heavy, screeching brakes and she stopped in her tracks and began chomping huge clumps of fur from her hind leg.

A downtown condo caught on fire in the middle of the afternoon and from our twelfth floor office windows we watched emergency vehicles burn down Michigan Ave. One of the account executives, a guy with a sickle scar down the length of his forearm, came back from a lunch meeting and said flames were bursting from windows like harpoons and even some balconies were on fire and the entire street was blocked off. Our boss appeared from his office, said the show was officially over, to get back to work, and made an O'Leary joke. I swallowed a caffeine pill and called a couple leads for small business accounts, and during one of the calls a fire engine and ambulance blazed by back-to-back and the potential customer on the phone asked me what was going on down there. I told him there was a fire downtown, in a condo building, with balconies on fire, and he said, "I just hope the city doesn't burn down before we can get some business done," and then we went right back to numbers. He asked if we offered small business loans too, which we did, and then asked about a home refinance. As we spoke, I logged the referrals into the system, told him I'd transfer him to business loans, who'd then transfer him over to mortgage, and if nobody answered they were probably already ash.

I had the hood of my sweatshirt over my head while I watched late-night TV and played tug-of-war with the dog. It was a '50s movie about a good, clean robbery, and the dog had a firm grip on her end of the rope, growling out of the side of her mouth and snapping her head from side to side like she was tearing meat off a carcass, her teeth stained from all her previous meals, and it came to me; her name was Z. She was the end of language, the finale of a string of known symbols, a last love. She scratched at the door and I put the TV on mute and grabbed her leash and we took a long walk past Graceland Cemetery, stopping on the sidewalk to look at the headstones in the warped streetlights, an ambulance howling up behind us, a block away, and she began twisting and kicking and somehow got her head free from her collar and bolted. I chased her, freaking like a father, screaming her name, but she slipped down an alley and out of sight. I knew she'd be okay because of the thick scar on her nose and the snap of her jaw, but I felt that old familiar feeling of missing something, so I walked around the neighborhood for a long time looking for her, swearing I saw her perked ears and muscular legs in some overgrown grass behind a surplus store, but it was just a pile of shredded truck tires. In the night quiet, I went to something primal, something like sonar, something animal, and suddenly I could hear the smallest sound of her, her footsteps a few blocks down, her hard panting, her far-away echo, and I ended up double-backing to the cemetery, and there she was on the sidewalk, smiling like a hooligan, and she let me put her collar back on.

I imagined a more productive tomorrow, feeling like an American man again. My stomach was growling and the only thing in my fridge was a dried-up tortilla, so I ripped the tortilla in two, ate half, and put the other half back. It was late evening, later than I usually got home from work, because Michael and I had gone to a downtown bar, a slapstick business joint, and drank a couple vodka orange juices. The window in my apartment had a new bb gun hole and I stood there and chewed and watched a kid with a baseball bat slam and shake the streetlight, my blood somehow repairing itself, pumping back into the bone, back into the brain valleys, because, earlier, on the L ride home from the bar, when I was resting my head against the window, the sunset chemical-vanilla, a man in the train humming what sounded like a hymn, the woman next to me, a nurse still in her scrubs, had pushed her hip against my hip, a slight smirk on her face, a brief exhale, so I'd inched my leg to the left to touch her leg and she'd inched her leg to the right to touch mine.

There were stenciled migraines all over her apartment walls, her collected paintings. It was a small apartment in a deteriorating neighborhood, with half the houses on the street boarded up and an abandoned firehouse across the street. I turned from the window and watched her drink her drink from across the room. She had leviathan hair, a dimple in her right cheek, and her bottom teeth were fallen soldiers. She said, "You're wasting your time with all that. I never think about death. What's the point?" I felt that love itch, and had a little weed left, so we stretched across her living room floor and smoked and listened to music, to some of her favorite songs. "I'm trying to be more honest lately, you know," she said. We eventually went to the bedroom and went sideways and she grabbed the back of my thigh and pushed her palm against my chest and I wrapped my hand around her calf and lifted her leg a little. I asked if it felt good and she said it felt pretty good. Her neck smelled like candlewax and I fell asleep with my hand on her rib cage, running my fingers up and down each rib. In the morning we went to a grocery store and while we stood in line she picked up a magazine and flipped through the pages. I wanted to tell her I loved her. I couldn't, didn't, though. But that's my only god: that love.

I was late to work, sweating my way up twelve flights because the elevator was out-of-order. Word around the water cooler was a shaft plunge, a suicide, and two people were absent from work that day, so we all imagined who it could be, which person was that sick of earth. Michael was one of the two missing, and because I hadn't heard from him in a while, and because his wife was still inside the sorrow of a stillborn birth, I worried he'd calculated the sum total of his suffering, decided to see if there was a next world, and jumped down the shaft. I texted him to see how everything was going, booted up my computer, immediately locked my screen, and went to the break room, where my boss was leaning his hip against the sink, drinking a cup of coffee. "Can you imagine if people had no job to go to? It would be anarchy. I bet suicides would be up like 45%," he said. I opened the refrigerator, but there was nothing for me inside, my boss coughing up something sinister without covering his mouth and leaving his coffee mug in the sink for somebody else to wash. And I washed his mug, concentrating on the water, the infinite ways the droplets could possibly be distributed from the faucet, the subtle changes in temperature, and after I'd filled up his mug with soapy water I stuck it in the freezer, behind some old Halloween candy, where I hoped it would freeze and shatter.

I waited at the bar, drinking a tomato juice, until Michael showed, his face a ragged blue. "Sorry to drag you down my way. I had to stop home. She swore she heard a crying sound," he said. He ordered a beer and then spun his glass in circles on the woodgrain. "I really think I'm going to have to quit and help her, or help her get some help," he said. "Her eyes are just dead." He drank the last of his beer and asked the bartender for another and then drank that one. The entire evening, he moved like a manufactured disease, with aches that seemed concrete chronic, his skinny wrists bending in unnatural ways. "It's only a job, only work. I don't want to come home one day and find out she's gone." A man at the end of the bar watched us like he knew the score, his Blackhawks hat tilted sideways, with sunglasses resting on the brim. Michael asked my opinion about the situation, if he should quit, if I thought she just needed time and he was overreacting, but I said I thought she needed help, told him I'd quit, if it were me, and I even told him I was probably going to quit soon too, but I didn't tell him why; I didn't tell him that, somewhere far off, like telepathy, I could feel Sarah in a private cloud of her own.

Michael's desk was empty and his papers were shredded and it was beautiful. The office was quiet that day, with keystrokes the heaviest sound, and I leaned back in my chair and looked at the windows of the neighboring skyscraper, the boxed pattern of fluorescents forming a crested star. "I took care of that boat loan for you. Just messed with some numbers. He's approved now," one co-worker said to another. Michael's empty desk was exactly what I wanted, so I went to my boss's office, an empty Tupperware container on his desk, lentil stained, and told him I quit in as few words as possible. He asked me if I'd received an offer from another bank, what I planned to do next, and what brought this whole deal on, but I didn't answer. I packed up my desk, my books and notebooks, my caffeine pills, shredded my paperwork, and two weeks later the final check was deposited into my account and I went to the grocery store and bought ten boxes of pasta for $10 and a whole host of olive oil.

Something was off in the mathematics of that night, a strange tilt to the moon or an extra spin of the earth, and there was no way in hard heaven I was falling asleep, so I threw off my blankets, grabbed my shoes, found Z's leash, and we went for a walk. We snuck down the back stairwell of the building so we wouldn't wake the neighbors, and the moment we hit the sidewalk Z's ears spun like radar and she titled her head sideways to sniff the air. She was pulling on her leash more than usual, pulling me past an automotive warehouse and across an intersection, until we were again walking on the sidewalk bordering Graceland Cemetery. In the city- filtered darkness I could see the outlines of angels and pyramids and crosses, and behind a gravestone shaped like a Naval ship I saw a fox, its thin silhouette barely visible in the streetlights, its eyes sparkling specks. Z let out a long, mournful howl I'd never heard from her before and the fox caught wind of us and ran off across the cemetery grounds and disappeared. We stood there for a few minutes, near the fence, trying to catch another glimpse of the fox, Z with her eyes wide open for any itch in the grass, but nothing else moved between the gravestones so we circled the block a couple times until we were both probably tired enough.

There was a protest downtown, after another summertime police shooting, a dead boy on the south side, the unrest perhaps becoming more than momentary, more than unorganized outrage. I opened all the windows in my apartment, but there was no wind, so I sat on the couch in a heavy humidity and found the tape I was looking for. I'd been labeling and relabeling all our foster father's recordings as their meanings changed. I played the tape and he spoke slowly like a dying battery. "I thought maybe it'd be a good thing in the long run. When I was drafted. I could go to college on the GI Bill if I made it back. And I wasn't up to too much at the time, anyway, just living in Detroit and working at a paint store. Detroit was happening back then though, in the mid-to-late '60s. People were moving there from all over because the jobs were good, the music was great, the nightlife was something else, and even the schools were good, so families were moving in. But when my number got called, I could actually see a positive side to going to Vietnam, like a college education and maybe some discipline, even though the discipline part is a bunch of bullshit. That's what they sell wayward kids on. The discipline." I glanced up at the TV, at the protests, and prepared myself to go downtown later to seethe. "And I'd known plenty of people, friends, who'd volunteered because they believed in that war, before they knew what was really going on, so there was still this thought that if I went we'd be doing something important, but that changed pretty much the moment we were in-country. What we think is going on is probably not really going on and most everything is a lie."

The future dug itself in and I was afraid I wouldn't be able to eat, so I gargled some mouthwash and tied my tie. The job, an entry-level advertising position, was only twenty or so blocks away, and I walked it in eighty-degree weather, my dress shirt sweated through and my shoes rubbing my heel to a blister about halfway there. The office was on the third floor of an old redbrick four-story that looked like it was designed by one of the Chicago Seven. It didn't have an elevator and I was out of breath as I stumbled into the small lobby of the agency. There was a futuristic logo, a hawk with neon talons, on the wall above the reception desk and the receptionist said my name before I could speak and told me to have a seat, her blouse something like strange black leather. She picked up the phone and spoke under her breath, in off-putting, slithering shades, her eyes darting away from me like it was all a secret, and then she chuckled and told the person on the line that she understood. She waved me up to the desk, looking at my shoes as I walked across the lobby, and while she pretended to type on her computer, her fingernails pointed and polished, she said they would have to reschedule, that something important had presented itself. She halfheartedly apologized and, tentatively, penciled me in for some time next week, and as I walked home I came up with some advertising slogans: We Can Reliably Orbital Drift Underwater, and Always Live Long With A Daisy Chain, and My Friend, Your Thirst Is Only Nylon, but I never got another interview.

Western Ave was a straight shot up to Evanston, a town north of Chicago, where the crowd thinned out and there weren't any skyscrapers, only five- or six-story office buildings and a university campus. The single-family homes seemed ripped right from grocery store magazines, with picket fences protecting small gardens and wrap around porches. Our foster mother had set me up on a blind date with Gina, adamant on the phone call that both Gina and I needed somebody, that we were too burned into our own heads, that we had some common ailments and interests, so I walked toward the coffee shop, through downtown Evanston, past a small dog tied to a parking meter, a couple salons, and a store that sold personalized gifts, ceramics and jewelry. At the coffee shop, Gina was sitting at an empty table, without a computer or books, even though she was a grad student. I was worried she'd know that I knew nothing at all. She saw me, a twitch of her left eye, and asked if I was who I was, and I said that I was, and we ordered coffee and sat there and talked, her sips a calculated self-control, so I tried to slow down my drinking. She had bright eyes and the kind of lips that sang. "So, I heard you got a rescue dog," she said. And she told me about her studies, her social work, her fundamental need to help people, and we talked about society, isolation, the parts we played, and when we finished our coffees we walked to her car, a small Chevy coupe with a cluttered backseat, and she asked if I wanted a ride back to the city, but I politely refused because I was already itching for the train.

It could've been the light, the oncoming evening storm refracting the streetlights, or it could've been that I was on no sleep again, but I'd been wandering around Uptown for hours under an ominous, vibrating, squealing sky. On a corner outside a closed bakery, a milk-white wedding cake in the window, I bumped into a woman I used to work with at the bank. She recognized me right away, excited about the coincidence, and I somehow remembered she had children. "They're doing pretty well. We thought Luke had leukemia," she said. "He's the middle one. He was lethargic and pale and vomiting. But when we took him to the hospital they said he just had a vitamin deficiency." In that storm light, her eyes were clothesline blankets, lightly swaying, and her gestures were too fluid, a water woman. She asked me how I was doing, said that everybody at the bank missed me, and I told her I was doing fine, that I was making my way. We said our goodbyes and I kept walking, eventually wandering into an open antique shop, where, near the cash register, a small radio played bebop. The man who worked there, a man with half a pinky finger, said the knife I was looking at was his longest-standing piece, that he'd bought it about twenty years ago from a man who was desperately selling everything he could. The handle was a green-bubbled jade, truly beautiful, but I told him I was too broke right now, that I'd be back another day, maybe.

The water dripping from my bathroom faucet appeared normal, but the drops had a strange weight to them, like small shotputs. I'd been holed up in my apartment for a week, my curtains closed and the doors dead-bolted, only sneaking Z out for her walks before dawn and after dark. Thousands of voices were there with me, speaking in unsaturated colors, in high vibrations, their words indecipherable, unintelligible, as though I were too close or too far to understand them. I swore one voice was our foster father behind the bedroom door with the tape recorder, and another Martha reassuring Boom Charlie he was good kid, and Sammy talking music with her little brother, even though he was gone, and Maggie dissecting a bottle, and I think I even heard the jazzman asking me if I had found that different kind of love yet. Just too many long-ago faces, so I called our foster mother a few times for help, and maybe for some money, or for another job connection, but she wasn't answering, so I closed my eyes and concentrated on a garbage truck lifting a dumpster and a wild catfight and a far-flung siren. I went to the bathroom to wash my face, the water dripping from the faucet now pooled at the bottom of the sink, solidified into something like clear molasses, and I scooped a handful and drank it down, hoping it would be my lottery, hoping it would form an onyx stone in my stomach and break me sincerely open.

Somewhere in the Chicago River there was the bloated body of a carpenter who'd got behind on a loan payment to the wrong people, who'd foolishly gambled his well-being, who'd took too much too easily, with lead poured inside his sliced open stomach. I could feel him like physics, but I'd also been drinking and smoking for a week straight, without a job, the lack of which was the second thing I thought about when I woke on a bench next to that river in the late afternoon, the sun hitting me in the face, a curdled flesh smell coming off the water, a decomposing once-human clump, the waterlogged skin of him, maybe, the carpenter. And soon, because of the hard heat, I was wide awake and panicked, about to puke, my leg asleep, dead numb. I sat up on the bench and massaged the back of my calf until it was pins and needles and then tried to stand, but my leg wouldn't respond, like it couldn't find my brain, so I limped down the river walk until I was forced to lean against a trashcan. Above the river, above the bridge, there was a skyscraper of a now defunct company, the tallest in the vicinity. I thought my muscles would never get back to normal, never regain full feeling, and that I'd be stuck in downtown Chicago, limping around, forever, but when I decided to try out my leg again it felt great, almost better than before, with no more pins and needles, so I simply got to walking.

Once a paper factory, with workers always out back during their smoke breaks, the company logo on their shirts, my sister and I often drifting past to ask for a cigarette or two, the building had now been converted into luxury lofts. The rear entrance was fixed with a new keypad lock, so I waited until someone left, a guy on his cellphone, and then slipped inside before it snapped shut. The stairwell was the same, still industrial, with a chemical sawdust smell, and I climbed it to the rooftop and pushed open the heavy metal door. And, in the brisk wind, I tried to remember, tried to recall that age, as I wandered around, looking down into skylights, a sleeping cat on a countertop, until I finally found the chimney I was looking for, the chimney with three missing bricks, but my sister's graffiti, an elderly hand holding a crowbar, was gone, probably power-washed away in the conversion. I checked all the other chimneys, but there was nothing, so I went to the edge of the rooftop and watched our old neighborhood swell in the dusk, a deep lie. In the distance, I could see the rear of the group home, which was repainted, and suddenly something stirred next to me, a small figure, a woman, difficult to see because she was wearing a black hooded sweatshirt. "Be careful, the roof gives out in spots," she said. And then, "Do you even live here?" She leaned a little closer to inspect, and I told her I was just looking for some old graffiti, my sister's. "I've never seen anything much up here other than pigeons, but what's her graffiti look like?" she said, so I told her about my sister's elderly hand crowbar graffiti, how it was a long time ago, and I told her my name. A skylight illuminated where we stood, and I let her study me, to gather my face, to show her I wasn't something deranged, and she eventually introduced herself as Sidney.

Silvia, our foster mother's housemate, called to tell me she thought our foster mother was acting strangely, that she was forgetting simple tasks, such as how to use the coffee maker, and forgetting simple words, like they were being erased. "I swear I heard her talking to someone in her bedroom a few nights ago, but nobody was in there. It sounded like sweet nothings," Silvia said. I told Silvia I'd be over soon, fed Z and refilled her water bowl, and hustled to the train. It was early afternoon and everybody on the L looked dried up. A man with one arm was walking around, asking for change, his shirtsleeve, tied in a knot at the cuff, hanging loose at his side. When the L jolted to a stop, I walked the ten blocks from the station to their apartment, buzzed, and, after a minute or two, Silvia came limping downstairs, dressed in a blue tracksuit, her hands shaking a little as she opened the door. She whispered about how our foster mother had forgotten to water the plants, too, that she'd forgotten to mention that on the phone. The apartment was freezing and our foster mother was in her bedroom, sitting in a rocking chair near the window, getting some sun and reading a book about Wall Street. As always, her bed was meticulously made, a quilt I recognized from the old apartment folded at the foot, a quilt Sarah used all the time. Our foster mother closed her book but continued to look out the window, her profile a lioness. "Silvia's just a worrier," she said. I cleared my throat and quietly asked if she'd been talking to herself, or to somebody else who wasn't here, if I should be worried. "Not any more than normal. I'm always talking to him." She turned to look at me and her face was thinner than last month and her lips had a new, small tremor she probably didn't know about, but she was herself, I could see that, still the same bluebird, just getting older.

It took two days to clean most of the mildew from my shower, but even with vinegar I couldn't dissolve the red ring around the drain. I also scrubbed down the entire kitchen, the sink, countertops, the crested stains on the stove, the inside and outside of the fridge, the small hairs in the compartments, the leaked sauces and such on the shelves. I burned lavender incense in the bedroom and took Z for a long walk so she wouldn't be insane for Sidney, and the dog brought back a stick she'd found on the sidewalk, proudly carrying it five or so blocks. She was chewing on her stick in the kitchen when Sidney called my cell, saying she was outside, but couldn't figure out which apartment was exactly mine. Downstairs, when she wasn't at the front door, I walked around the corner to find her standing outside another building, checking her phone, and we hugged and I probably knew. Before we went into the apartment, I told her about Z, about her scars and muscles, that she looked intimidating but was rarely aggressive. "I love any dog, especially the tough ones. We all have our pasts," she said, which was good, because the minute we walked through the door Z was all over her, huffing at her in deep breaths like a hound, especially at her boots. Sidney kneeled to pet Z, her bag sliding off her shoulder to the kitchen floor, exposing some contents, and Z slowly calmed to her touch and then followed her around for the rest of the night. "The window glass is warped. I like it," Sidney said. She took of her boots and we sat on the couch, sharing as much as we needed to, me not daring to turn on the TV, her telling me about how calcium in the most abundant metal in the human body, how we probably even have bones in our bellies, belly bones. She got up to use the bathroom, and when she came out laughing, asking me about the ceiling, I told her it'd all caved in last winter.

After we left the bar, without drinking, only eating a lunch of spinach dip and tortilla chips, Sidney and I decided to go see a movie at Navy Pier. "I haven't been there since I was a kid. My mom took me on a whim. We ended up seeing this movie about pilots in a war. I used to dread going to war when I was younger," she said. I wanted to catch a cab to the pier, to get the royal treatment, but we ended up taking the L, which was crowded that Saturday, Sidney and I slammed against a window, a Bears game beginning in a couple hours. Florida was on my mind, even though I was having second thoughts, because of her; Sidney was a burgeoning oasis. But $29.99 for all available online records, Sarah living in a swamp, the mosquitos keeping her up all night, filling up on her blood, and I needed to kill some living ghosts. I thought there was no better time, on our way to a movie, Sidney and I smashed together, our faces inches apart, her eyes this rich dirt, a touch of hands, the L somehow always an aphrodisiac, to ask her if she could watch Z for a week or so while I took a trip. She barely even thought about it. "It'll be good for me. Yeah, I will. You better come back, though. You're pretty much leaving your dog with a stranger," she said. I told her I'd be back, that I knew it was a big ask, but I had a good feeling about it, a certain feeling, and that I'd leave meticulous instructions. A woman next to us on the L was smiling as she listened to our conversation, like kindness was worth watching, and as the train slowed, Sidney finally asked me where I was going, and I told her Florida, and that it was important. The movie we saw was in 3D, Sidney and I wearing our glasses, uncomfortably ticking inside our clothes when an onscreen love scene barreled right for us.

I caught a train at Union Station and lounged in a window seat with the hood of my sweatshirt pulled over my head. The glass was plastered with humanoid oil and the city looked like a hard dream as it disappeared. I wanted to see something memorable before leaving Chicago, something to call me back, besides Z and Sidney, like a protest-engulfed neighborhood, with smoke rising, or kids cracking open a fire hydrant and dancing in the street, or a crashed airplane burning wingless in the middle of Michigan Ave, but soon the city was gone, and the land turned open and flat, with wind turbines spinning on low, grassy plains. The lull of the train finally drained my eyes and I halfheartedly slept, half-waking to see a rust belt town pass, its main street nearly deserted, the windows of its three-story buildings either boarded up or with air-conditioners hanging out, and a falcon, or maybe a hawk, hovering over a pickup truck in an out-of-business gas station parking lot. The man next to me whispered to himself and I swallowed more sleeping pills and woke just as the train split Charleston, WV in two, with its gold-domed capitol building where Lincoln walks at midnight, and I unstuck my face from the window and the man next to me had already moved seats.

The Atlantic waves were crashing in like cannons and I picked up a coiled seashell and carved our foster father's name in the sand with its edge, an ocean liner, out on the horizon, bending on the breakers, the clouds beginning to descend and turn dark, with most everyone on the beach packing up their umbrellas and leaving, but I needed the rain. I imagined a Florida hurricane, with palm trees torn from the ground and thrown like javelins across viaducts, lampposts sucked airborne, a Saffir-Simpson wind ripping me straight off the shore and hurling me headfirst into the windshield of an expensive car, maybe a Mercedes, where I'd bleed to death, stuck in the shattered glass. The sky soon was plum evil so I walked down the beach toward a not-too-distant pier, sand crusted in my hair and inside my shirt, a needle rain splintering my neck. There was a small tiki bar at the end of the pier with what looked like shelter and as I approached, the bartender, who was watching a small TV, asked me what I wanted, and I told him everything. I drank under the straw roof, really drank, the storm turning even more ominous, the waves transforming from cannons into something more automatic, the bartender and I talking about standup comedians and money, the TV on the news, showing another shooting.

A berserk pride of peacocks sauntered down the middle of the road, holding up traffic, one car swerving to avoid them, another car honking its horn until the birds slowly made their way to the median. I found an entrance to the beach and on a sand dune, near a patch of gnarled brush, wiry animal fur tangled on the thorns, I stretched out in the x-ray sun for a couple hours, watching bodyboarders and cargo ships, my face skin searing. The heat eventually suffocated me and I shook off the sand and walked further down the beach, toward shade and wind, toward a fisherman with his pole stuck upright in the sand, his line out in the ocean, a mesh trap of some sort in his hand. He watched me as I stumbled in boots, knowing I wasn't a Floridian, and I took a winding path past a conglomeration of condo buildings, and at the end of the path, near a private road, there was a trashcan, and inside, on top of a pizza box, was a bloodied beach towel, the stains deep, the fabric nearly soaked through. Maybe it was another snake, like my sister had found, so I searched the surrounding grass and found a stick and stirred at the towel like a pot until I saw what was really wrapped inside. Back in my motel room, where the TV remote smelled like wet meat and my ankle itched from strange bites, I tried to fall asleep, but instead, in some spectral gesture, I somehow rose from my body and floated across town, to that beach, to that trashcan, where I entered the body of what was wrapped in that towel, that mangled, wingless, legless seabird and oddly there was no pain at all.

In the motel room, in the nightstand drawer, there was a brochure for the space coast, with a star bound rocket on the front flap, and as I watched TV I flipped through some factoids about the space program, how six Apollo missions had landed on the moon, how a satellite is any object that travels around another object. On the local news, a man had gone missing from a retirement home, a car had caught fire in an Orlando parking garage, burning other cars with it, and a tropical storm was headed for the gulf. My hunger was shaping me and I tossed the brochure on the bed, took a quick shower, decided to go unshaven, and walked a few blocks to a restaurant in a strip mall. The buffet was all starch, the heat lamps an unnatural orange, and I sat there and watched people eat, most of them never looking up from their plates, one couple in the corner sharing a newspaper article, maybe a heartwarming story about orphans. I ate an egg roll and scrolled through phone numbers in my cell, streamlining my contacts, reliving memories associated with certain names. I only deleted two numbers, Mary and Mia, thought about Sidney and Z, and finished what I could of my rice. Outside the sun was tinfoil and I ran across the street and ducked back inside the motel lobby, where I filled a paper cup with water and recovered in the air-conditioning, a family of four straggling in to rent a room, the youngest child reaching up to ring the bell at the front desk, so proud that he was growing.

It was prehistoric as hell down there, the highway canals lurking with predators. I wrapped my t-shirt around my head to stop the sun from peeling my skin away and walked the shoulder of a causeway, searching every face I could, from every angle, for Sarah. Above, the birds were clawed rainbows circling, and I had to step around a dead, burst armadillo on the pavement, its pale, naked tail curled behind its body as a feeler, and I hoped my sister, wherever she was, could see me out there suffering, see the wounds on my face, the heat coming off the road in terrible waves, the gators lying in wait for my dehydrated collapse, the drifting roadside killers. I climbed a guardrail to get off the main road and went down a sun-scorched hill, across a dry canal, and snuck my way into a gated community, a focused subdivision, where I sat on a park bench next to a manmade pond. A woman and two children were eating at a picnic table across the water, but the woman wasn't her. She was about the same age as Sarah, but too tall and too inauspicious. She looked over at me a couple times, probably thinking I was a vagrant, but soon her attention went back to one of the children, who had dropped the plastic spoon from his sundae straight in the sand.

In the dead middle of the night, an Atlantic wind twisting the palm trees, the entire room, the entire motel, the entire town began to shake in a disturbed, air raid way. Dogs barked outside and everything loose rattled and I grabbed hold of the bed, a nuclear event going through my head, our living end, and soon the shaking intensified, becoming a kind of chopping reverberation, an extremity fever, and then what sounded like a missile burned overhead. I rushed outside and there were already a few people standing around in the parking lot, looking skyward, but whatever it was, any trace of it, was gone. A kid in pajamas clutched the leg of a man I presumed to be his father and I walked over to talk to them, but before I could say a word, he asked me, "What in Saint Sebastian shit was that?" I said I had no idea, all three of us staring up at a clear night with a few static stars, salt and the sea in the wind. I told him I'd go find out and inside the motel lobby, which was empty, except for the night clerk, who was stocking small cereal boxes for tomorrow's breakfast, I asked if we'd just been attacked, and the night clerk, seeing the look on my face, a half-fearful, half-relieved nuclear apocalypse dumb stare, said, "Just a satellite. They send them up all the time." When I asked him what kind of satellite it was, he just shrugged and started stocking again, so I went back outside to tell the man and his son that we were probably safe, that now we'd have better foreign intel or better cellphone service or a way to capture license plates from space, but they'd already gone back inside their motel room.

It was my sister's last listed address, the apartment complex jumbo, with at least eight different buildings separated by half-empty parking lots, some of the spaces covered by overhangs to shield cars from sun and salt. The buildings on the west side of the complex ran along the length of a canal, the water heavy with green gunk and palm leaves, infested, one of the canals you see on a local news story about a small dog getting snatched from the embankment. In the parking lot, I checked my reflection in the tinted window of a white coupe, combed my hair, and wiped the corners of my mouth clean, the sun somehow slithering inside my neck, her address in my pocket, memorized. When I finally found her building, I walked up to the third-floor apartment and looked in the window. The shades were closed and at first there were only vibrations, a child's voice, a question or two called out, but then I saw her through the slats, sitting on the floor in the middle of the room, watching TV, dressed in cartoon pajamas, eating a popsicle, her curly hair. I closed my eyes and I swear I heard my sister's voice, heard her answer the little girl's question.

My nerves were about to squeeze me unconscious, so I staggered down the stairs, left my sister's apartment complex, and walked a hard mile uphill until I realized there was nothing the way I was going. Something smelled like burning pickles and the high sky was dusted with dissolving shapes, my eyes bubbling to a blur. In the distance, I thought I saw some shade, a respite, but as I approached it was just a stripped cypress tree hanging over the potholed road. My phone vibrated in my pocket and when I checked the number it read as a riddle, a sequence of numbers that spelled an invitation. I felt a camera on me, a pronged air, and shame. A truck revved its engine somewhere and I followed the sound of it down a winding street and through an overgrown greenbelt, and when I came out of the weeds there was a gas station on the corner. The child in that apartment, if it was Sarah's place, could be novel, a fresh layer of dirt. I bought a bottle of water in the gas station and chugged it, the phone vibrating in my pocket again, and outside, before I threw the bottle away, I checked the trashcan for anything in need of saving.

Through a gap in the shades the little girl looked like my sister, with olive skin and long limbs, and I waited for her to turn away from the TV so I could see her eyes, but she didn't budge from her show. I was a caught thorn, an itching slice, and I eventually willed the strength to knock, and when I snuck back to the window, the girl was staring directly at me, and she was it, our fresh layer. She called for her mother and soon the deadbolt unlocked and the door opened and Sarah, older now, with sunbaked skin, stood there, stoic like she was expecting me. "I'll be right back. Keep watching TV," my sister said and shut the apartment door, grabbing my wrist and pulling me aside and away from where the girl could see us through the window. "I knew you were close. I even just called. Remember when I said I'd need you when I really needed you." Sarah pulled a pack of cigarettes and a lighter from the pocket of her sweatpants and lit one. I was being buried face down in darkness as she told me she was having trouble, the same kind of trouble as our mother, that she'd been locking herself in a room for hours and unrolling spools of fabric and trying to cut them into perfect circles. "I've slowly become an uncontrollable impulse. Like her with the wallpaper," she said. "I think I need to go to the hospital, James. I need to go to the hospital and you need to take care of Nina."

Sarah gave me the keys to her Chevy something and we drove to the hospital, which was just outside Orlando, little Nina in the backseat, barely making a sound the entire ride, the girl just staring out the window with a raggedy stuffed crocodile on her lap. At the hospital, we unloaded Sarah's two backpacks, unbuckled little Nina, and as we walked toward the entrance my sister said, "When I get called, I want to go in there myself. I don't want Nina to know about this yet. And after I'm in there, take her somewhere as a distraction. She likes anything with paintings or food. I'll call you as soon as I can." We sat in the waiting room, little Nina like a ceramic mime, tracing shapes in the air with her small, unscarred hands, circles and diamonds and spirals, my sister tracing shapes back to her like they were speaking a lost language. A man with oxygen tubes in his nose and his head bandaged was being pushed in a wheelchair across the waiting room, and little Nina watched his every breath, her eyes globes. A nurse called my sister's name and Sarah grabbed her backpacks and gave Nina a long hug, kissed her forehead, and whispered something in her ear, something that sounded like strength. Sarah told me to make sure my phone was always charged and followed the nurse back into the corridors of the hospital. Little Nina made what looked like the shape of a sun with her hands, and I asked her if I could hold her hand, and she reached for mine, and we walked back to the car, which was scorching inside, the steering wheel sticky from the heat. We listened to the radio, a morning block of pilgrimage tunes, as we drove home. "See that place with the black and red umbrellas outside? A man who works there has an eye patch. Can we go?" little Nina said. It was a café on a sharp corner and I pulled into the parking lot and went around to unbuckle little Nina and when I lifted her she was heavier than I'd imagined.

The park was overgrown with buffalo grass and the swing-set was sun-bleached and little Nina and I rested on a bench and ate ice cream. I told her the story about Jimmy, the mechanic, but I don't think she was listening. A dinosaur of a bird swirled above us and my phone vibrated in my pocket and when I answered my sister's voice was faint. "I'm in for overnight observations. They are worried about me, the auditory and visual hallucinations especially," she said. Little Nina watched my face as I listened, the ice cream from her cone dripping down her hand. "It won't be too long, hopefully. And Nina's self-sufficient for her age. She knows what she needs and wants and once she's asleep she's asleep. Where did you take her?" I told Sarah we were in a park eating ice cream, and that I'd also taken her to the eye-patch-man café. My sister asked to talk to her, and I gave the phone over to little Nina, and she handed me her melting ice cream cone. The bird, its wingspan behemoth, swung over the water while I tried to sneak a listen to their conversation, which had to be dark hole for both of them, but especially for my sister, who had to attempt to explain her brain to a child, to admit illness, which was something our own mother had never done. Little Nina kissed the phone and handed it back to me, but sister had already hung up. I wasn't sure what to do, so we walked the park for another half-hour, little Nina finding some kind of Florida wildflower with a sticky stem and miniscule petals.

Little Nina said it was the key with the purple sticker and I unlocked the front door of their apartment and she stood in the doorway, listening for a few seconds like she was expecting an intruder. The apartment was clean, mother-daughter minimalist, except for the kitchen counter, which was cluttered with unopened mail. Nina saw me looking at the mail and said, "Mom never opens letters. She says none of them are ever seashells or sand." She asked me if I wanted to see the rest of the apartment and the first place she showed me was what she called "Mom's chaos room." It was a small bedroom with spools of fabric – velvets and silks and lace – strung across the floor. Much of the fabric had been cut into shapes, mostly spirals and circles, and the shapes had been stapled to the walls. The window was completely covered with an old bedsheet and there must have been ten different ashtrays in there, all filled with smoked cigarettes. "Sometimes we sleep in here. When our beds are full of blasted rats," little Nina said. The next room she showed me was her bedroom, and there was a small, unmade bed in the corner and a makeshift cinderblock nightstand with a brass lamp on top. Also on the nightstand was a stack of papers, and little Nina grabbed them to show me. There was a foot without any toes, a rocket pack scuba-diver, and a toad sitting on a cracked mirror. "We trade. I draw a curious scene and then Mom draws a curious scene. It's just a big stack of scenes," she said. "Maybe tonight you can draw one and I can draw one and we'll trade too." I asked her why her walls were bare, why she didn't have any posters or anything, like her mother used to, but she ignored the question and walked out to the hallway to show me a shut door slaughtered with scuffs, the wood around the doorknob shaved away. Little Nina said it was her mom's room and nobody was allowed in there, not even her brother, because it was a pure sanctuary.

I woke on the couch in the middle of the night, the apartment a ghost in a rocking chair, invisibly creaking, and for a moment I forgot where I was, forgot I wasn't alone like usual, but the absence of the L, and the sound of wildlife outside, an opossum screaming like it was being ripped open, brought me back. I checked my phone and there was a text from Sidney saying Z had done well at a dog park, except for when another dog had tried to hump her, that she'd gone straight for that dog's throat, and Sidney had to break it up. I texted her back and then went down to little Nina's room and cracked open the door, the brass lamp on her cinderblock nightstand a mellow glow, her blankets strung across the bed and her sketches scattered on the floor, but she was gone. My chest became a thumping pain as I imagined all kinds of senseless danger, like a man creeping in through the window while I was asleep to steal her, or a call on her cellphone that she'd answered, a tempting voice pretending to be someone it wasn't, asking her address, luring her outside to coax her into a tinted-window sedan and creep off. But soon, after turning on all the lights in the apartment and scrabbling in disarray, I found her asleep on the floor of the chaos room with a few sheets of her mother's fabric covering her.

Little Nina was asking me all kinds of questions, like if I'd had to leave my family behind in order to take care of her, if I was going back to Chicago after this, if I was named after my father, if I had a father, but I didn't tell her much because Sarah had texted me to be careful with our past, that it was Nina's main curiosity. Instead, I told her about Sammy and the symphony, how we were dressed, how she was my first, beautiful love. "Is that something splendid? Yes, it is. That is something very splendid," little Nina said as she sat on a stool at the kitchen counter and watched me cook rice on the stove. When the rice was done, she grabbed a pamphlet about hang-gliding from the pile of mail on the counter and read it as she ate. I asked her if she needed salt or hot sauce or something else, but she just ate her rice plain, her eyes changing shape as the apartment filled with Florida sun. She took a drink of water and looked straight at me like she could read my entirety. "Mom says my dad got lost in something people sometimes get lost in," she said, scratching the bridge of her nose like she had a tickle. "She also says he will probably never become unlost. I've never met him either." I sat next to her and ate my rice, putting a few drops of hot sauce on it, and when little Nina saw that, she grabbed the bottle and shook so much sauce on her rice it tinted red. She took a bite and her face wrinkled. I told her it was strong stuff, to be careful, but she took another gigantic bite and chewed it slow and strong.

Little Nina asked if her friend Marcus, from downstairs, could come up and paint. I texted my sister and about an hour later she texted back, saying she'd call Marcus's mother, but it *was a flash in the pan.* Overnight her texts had become progress-sively jumbled, probably from the drugs, with strange metaphors, like *mothers are always such a limelight* and *I was a wilted mountain before.* I told little Nina what her mother had said regarding Marcus and she went to the bathroom, brushed her teeth, and got dressed, choosing a purple t-shirt with a black dragon on the front. In the living room, she sat in a spot of sun with her eyes closed, her stillness and silence unnerving. My sister texted back that Marcus would be up soon. *But, if you can, I mean it's important, don't let them paint the walls. Sometimes they do that, like almost every time. Two kids holding stopwatches.* There was a knock on the door and when I opened Marcus stood there with balled-up fists, giving me the once over. He yelled downstairs to his mom that everything was cool and an apartment door slammed shut. "You're burnt. Wear sunscreen. It's Florida," he said, strolling into the apartment to sit next to little Nina, who was still on the floor with her eyes closed, but smirking now. She scooted over to a drawer in the TV stand and pulled out some paints and construction paper and I stood at the kitchen counter, pretending to read the hang-gliding pamphlet, and watched them paint with heavy strokes. "Yours looks like snake fungus," little Nina said. "It's a herd of dangerous pigeons," Marcus said. And they painted for an hour and then Marcus washed his hands in the bathroom sink and went back downstairs and little Nina asked if the paintings were good enough for a museum.

She barely slept, the suction of her bare feet ticking across the apartment most of the night, the girl hovering next to where I tried to sleep on the couch. I whispered to her that it may run in the family, the sleep, and she let out a soft breath. It had to be three in the morning, and the complex was quiet except for the sound of a pair of high-heeled shoes in the parking lot. "What if she never comes home?" little Nina said. It was our hereditary worry. I said that her mom would be back, that she was a fighter, that she had no idea how hard her mom had battled to just be here, that she'd probably be back with even more love and maybe a little less chaos, but, I said, no matter what, no matter what, someone, me and Z, would be there to take care of her. And I remembered our birth mother, and how she'd disappear for a week to see a dog about a man, and how she'd come home with bags under her eyes and a sour sinister smell on what was left of her clothing, and little Nina rustled to the floor, laid parallel to the couch, and rubbed her bare feet together, so I gave her my blanket. "Mom said Chicago has rich museums. If she doesn't come back, can we go? I like any painting with a blue body." Soon her breathing calmed to a pattern, like her mother's, and she was still, but I stayed up the rest of the night because I thought that if I fell asleep, she'd wake.

My sister called and said she'd probably be out in a couple days, that she'd been sleeping, the medication seemed to be working, and the doctor felt confident that she wasn't a harm. "How's my daughter?" she said, and I told her Nina was in her bedroom looking at her and Marcus's paintings for the tenth time. "When you come get me, don't bring her inside again. They'd probably reconsider releasing me if they knew I had an eight-year-old. I told the doctor I only have myself to worry about. And don't make her any promises either. Just in case a couple days turns into a week." I made pasta and little Nina and I watched a show about exaggerated seeds while we ate, and after lunch she asked if we could drive around. I let her buckle herself in and we cruised, looking for ice cream or trouble, I said, which made her smile. It was a salt and fire day, the locals out on their bikes, many of them only wearing swimsuits, their tanned bare feet curled on the pedals. "Is digging a hole trouble?" little Nina asked. "How about picking up a turtle and putting it in the tall grass. Or how about kissing a monster?" I told her it depended how deep the hole was, where the turtle wanted to be, and how long the kiss was. I pulled into a gas station to put a few dollars' worth in my sister's car, the money she'd left us running low and my money almost gone, and then we drove along the coast, the ocean sparkling to the left, some blues on the radio, little Nina's eyes slowly closing. I watched her sleep in the rearview mirror, her head resting on her left shoulder and her hair sweaty, but she wasn't out for long and soon her eyes popped open and she said, "Is wishing for something a kind of trouble too?"

It was revolutionary, the way my sister looked walking out of the hospital, her eyes bright sails, her hair washed, her skin smooth, and she'd put on some weight. Little Nina saw it too and began to twist in her car seat as her mother approached. *Useful insanity is an act of rebellion*, my sister had texted me one night from the hospital. Sarah opened the door, bent down, and kissed Nina, whispering something new in her ear, something that sounded like a magical apology, and the little girl began to cry small tears. "Let's just go home," Sarah said. There was still some sticky residue where the IV had been taped to her arm and I turned out of the hospital parking lot and we drove home slowly, the three of us silent, trying to capture whatever we were feeling, that soft peace, the sun loud decibels and the car soaked with our smells, Sarah grabbing a pair of sunglasses from the center console, looking back at her daughter to smile as she did, a folder full of paperwork on her lap, prescriptions and all.

They were cleaning out the chaos room while I made pasta – olive oil, garlic, and spinach. I'd tried to keep the apartment exactly how Sarah had left it. I hadn't stepped foot in her bedroom, hadn't touched anything behind the bathroom mirror, the pills or oils, hadn't broken a bowl or misplaced a spoon, hadn't opened or thrown away any of the mail on the kitchen counter, even the religious magazines that were addressed to the previous tenant. When what our birth mother called pasta Randazzo was done, I yelled for them, and Sarah and little Nina came out of the chaos room with armfuls of fabrics and tossed it all in a heap at the front door. They grabbed their bowls and sat at the kitchen counter to eat, the two of them looking like divided halves of a single cell, both with their scratched-up elbows and marble eyes. "It tastes like a volcano," little Nina said. My sister nodded in agreement, and once she'd chewed and swallowed, Sarah said, "Like Mount Edna." After dinner, on the couch, we watched a primetime show about upper-class electricity and little Nina's eyes drifted shut and she fell asleep with her head in her mother's lap. "When are you going back?" my sister whispered, and I looked straight ahead at the TV and tried to think. I told her whenever she wanted me to go back, and little Nina shifted in her sleep like she was listening. "I feel like I need some peace and quiet. That's all," Sarah said, and I said whatever she needed.

I hugged Nina and her eyes they were dryer than mine, only faintly damp, the little girl tough as statues. The apartment smelled like orange vanilla incense and all the mail on the counter was opened and organized and the chaos room was orderly and I'd made a couple days' worth of pasta and stored it in the fridge for them. My sister unlocked the front door and leaned in and hugged me, something I'd been waiting for, and whispered, "If you weren't here, she could've become like us. That day on the street. I wasn't ready for you to know." A cab was waiting in the parking lot to take me to the train station. "I have a new person," little Nina said, and I nearly lost what little strength I had, so I grabbed my bag and went downstairs. Inside the cab, as we pulled away, I looked up at my sister's apartment and she and little Nina were standing on the landing, my sister's arm on the girl's shoulder, their faces sublime. The cab driver saw me in the rearview mirror, saw the crumbling state I was in, and asked, "You going home or leaving home?" And I swallowed the lump in my throat and told him I was going to D.C.

When I got to D.C., the train a long wilderness with an abrupt stop in a Carolina because a man had a medical emergency on board, an undone organ, I let my spinal fluid unwind and bought a bottle of water at the gift shop. I wandered past the statue of Themis and then left the station, the street outside pure butchery, the heart in leisurely destruction, a gasoline stink, and I searched for signs indicating landmarks, stopping on a sidewalk in front of a tax firm, where a delicate spider web hung across the window, bisecting an advertisement for crisp money. Wanting only to vibrate it to see what creeped out, I gently touched a tendon of the web, but the whole thing came undone and curled around my finger, so I washed the web away with a drip from my water bottle and followed group of tourists around the city, the visitors speaking in electric language, stripping off layers of clothing; and soon it appeared right there in front of us, the three-story, eleven-bay Palladian. I'd thought about, imagined, for so long, scaling that wall and running in a free sprint across the lawn, dodging whatever they threw at me, tear-gas and bullets, until I made it to the Oval Office, where I'd shatter headfirst through the window and bum-rush the premises. I'd find a piece of broken glass shaped like a silver dollar and slice the President clockwise across the throat before the Secret Service arrived and then there'd be a shin against my spine and handcuffs, but I'd be alive, I imagined.

A man took rapid-fire pictures with quick mechanical clicks while, next to him, a woman read from a guidebook about how soldiers had once set it on fire. I could feel it, the tenuousness of the place. It was already just a ruin in a marsh. "We protect each other here," Martha had said once, as she searched our room in the home, my sister protesting the invasion. The man turned his camera on me, and I knew; I knew my skin was burned and peeling and my eyes were hooked worms. I knew that whatever had been building inside was written all over, so I understood when he clicked off a few pictures of me. He then turned his camera back to the White House, his teeth a gold-rush tin pan, the woman next to him still reading from the guidebook, reading about how the architect wasn't even an American and it was built by slaves.

I circled around to another section of fence because I'd been standing in the same spot for too long, and the satellites, the Secret Service on the roof, the man with his camera, would soon think me more than a tourist. A charter busload of people, the license plate from Arkansas, unloaded at the curb and the occupants wandered out, unaccustomed to capitol productions, eventually clumping together in small groups on the sidewalk. From that angle, outside the west-side fence, the White House looked like a talon in amber, almost impossibly kept, the windows bulletproof. In front of me a teenager grabbed the fence and started shaking the metal bars, just like I wanted to, but in a flash a woman pulled him aside and gave him a quiet talking-to, a discreet scolding. I lit a cigarette and wondered which window was the Lincoln bedroom, staring at the house for as long as I could without blinking, trying not to flinch in the face of it.

I let the White House alone and went to a cafe and waited like Princip. I thought about our foster father, about how he carried himself with calm at the end, and I thought about war. My cellphone was low battery, but I called our foster mother, who didn't answer, she and Silvia probably out on a Saturday afternoon, shopping for books and fabric, stopping for lunch at a favorite patio restaurant, where they'd watch young mothers push children around in strollers. I checked my pockets for crumpled bills and loose change and picked up the menu. The waiter came over, his eyes on me like infrared, studying my skin, the blisters, the fresh scar above my eyebrow, the stains on my hooded sweatshirt. I was cordial, probably overly polite, feeling as though I'd overstepped my bounds, but when I asked him for only water, he said I had to order something. I only had enough money for the train back to Chicago, if I was going back, back to what I was, or maybe I'd go someplace new, invent a name, mask my face, or maybe I'd build a new history, travel, visit Dante's tomb with Sidney, or I could just jump the fence, which was the way I was leaning, or, you know, I could simply disappear myself.

The Amtrak scorched through the south side, the skyline visible now, a toothed horizon, the man sitting next to me clicking the locks on his briefcase over and again, mumbling something about liquidity, how we only congeal where we happen to be, like caged jelly. I pulled my backpack from under the seat and searched through it for my sunglasses. In the front pocket I found a sheet of folded construction paper, a little Nina painting, but I thought I'd wait until I got home to see what she'd painted. The man next to me licked his index finger and tried to scrub a scuff off his black dress shoe. He opened his briefcase and inside there were a few folders, color-coded, an unopened pack of ballpoint pens, a granola bar, and a phone charger. He saw me looking so he snapped it shut and the train curved around industrial swampland and already I could feel the past again.

Little Nina called the minute I walked into my apartment. Like she was a genetic bloodhound and could now track me across state lines. "Did you find the painting in your backpack? It's us, small and powerful," she said. I told her I'd found it, that it was a brilliant likeness, a humble but galvanizing scene, and that I planned to hang it somewhere in my apartment, when I found the perfect spot. She then asked what it was like in Chicago, so I described the scaffolding and skyscrapers, the train and its graffiti, the masks and money. "I hope I can visit. Mom said it's where our history is," she said. My apartment felt like a dead thing preserved, and I stood at the window and watched a man carry a couple black plastic bags from the liquor store down the street while little Nina talked about her new paintings, how she did one of the eye-patch man at the cafe, and one of Marcus's new basketball shoes, a red, technological pair, and one that took her a long time, of that man at the hospital in the wheelchair with oxygen tubes in his nose, and another of me and her mother, when we were young, that she saw us, somehow, on the couch together, watching a show about ribbons and wallpaper, and a man and two women were also in the room, but she didn't paint the other three people because she couldn't quite glimpse them.

At the paper factory, Sidney buzzed me up to the fifth floor, and when I knocked on the door Z barked somewhere in the apartment. Sidney answered flustered and inflamed and said, "I had to lock her in the bedroom. She's been an absolute pain all day." I apologized for the behavior, and thanked her again for watching Z, that it was no small feat, Sidney eyeing the patch of peeled skin on my forehead, a raw, wishbone-shaped mystery for her to solve, maybe. Her apartment, which was rearranged slightly since I saw it last, after the 3D movie, us love crashed, was a carved-out loft, with high ceilings and five mismatched chairs in the shape of a star in the main room. Z barked and scratched at the door so I asked Sidney if she was ready for madness and opened the bedroom and Z blasted out and began circling me, jumping backwards when I made any movement towards her, low growling like I was a vile stranger. I said her name and she sniffed at my shoes and once she recognized me she jumped up and slammed her paws against my chest. "So how was your pilgrimage? What did you do down there?" Sidney asked. I told her it was a good trip, something cathartic, something so I could move forward, but from her eyes I knew she wanted me to tell her more, so I told her about the dead bird in the trashcan in Florida, and how I'd stopped in D.C., and how the White House seemed the same as the bird. I petted behind Z's ears and touched the scar on her nose and Sidney pulled a treat from her pocket, a baked peanut butter ring, and Z snatched it away. I asked Sidney if she'd be interested in going out Thursday night, if she wanted to wander around and live our remaining lives. "There's always an exhibition downtown. That'd be perfect," she said.

"Nights, when we were getting ready for bed, when we were shaking the dust and hair from our blankets and punching our pillows soft, I'd try to guess what your mother was going to dream about, and she'd try to guess what I would. Once in a blue moon we had the same kind of dream, maybe a dream about our collapsed home being reassembled, something with hope, a home where all the faces were faces we wanted to know, to remember, beautifully ugly like gnarled trees, a home where you were perfect from the moment you were born, despite the outside. Your mother, I think, Nina, she dreamed of a place, a home, where you could rest your head on anyone's shoulders and think, 'If I fall asleep here, nobody will hurt me,' but even then she and I, even as children, we knew our dreams were absurd, that the world was close to the opposite, and if you wanted a home like that you'd have to imagine it."

"Like together dreams. You and mom. I like that one. Some I like, and some I don't really like," little Nina said. I was on the phone with her, on the couch, with the hood of my sweatshirt over my head, the city an ancient drum, Z next to me, her pointed ears pinned back and twitching but her eyes drifting closed as she fought sleep. It was late evening and little Nina had been calling me almost every night, often on speakerphone so her mother could talk and listen. "Her teacher hung one of her paintings in the classroom. It was a nuclear bomb family. Right, Nina?" my sister said from some distant place in her apartment, her voice static depth. "An atom bomb family," little Nina corrected. She asked her mother if she could bring the phone to her bedroom because she was getting tired, and my sister said as long as she only talked to me and didn't answer any strange calls from strangers with strange numbers. I said goodnight to Sarah and little Nina put me on hold while she changed into her pajamas and when she was ready for bed we talked quietly about how she'd lost a tooth, how it felt like an open door, and how she and her mother had been going for early morning runs around the complex, to exercise for sanity, she said, and how on one of those runs they saw a sunrise with feathers, a sweet bird so early, and soon her voice began to tire and fade and she told me to tell her the sparks and skyscrapers story again, her favorite one, the one where the kids burn everything to the ground, and I think we both fell asleep.

about atmosphere press

Atmosphere Press is an independent, full-service publisher for excellent books in all genres and for all audiences. Learn more about what we do at atmospherepress.com.

We encourage you to check out some of Atmosphere's latest releases, which are available at Amazon.com and via order from your local bookstore:

Until the Kingdom Comes, poetry by Jeanne Lutz
Warcrimes, poetry by GOODW.Y.N
The Freedom of Lavenders, poetry by August Reynolds
Convalesce, poetry by Enne Zale
Poems for the Bee Charmer (And Other Familiar Ghosts), poetry by Jordan Lentz
Serial Love: When Happily Ever After... Isn't, poetry by Kathy Kay
Flowers That Die, poetry by Gideon Halpin
Through The Soul Into Life, poetry by Shoushan B
Embrace The Passion In A Lover's Dream, poetry by Paul Turay
Reflections in the Time of Trumpius Maximus, poetry by Mark Fishbein
Drifters, poetry by Stuart Silverman
As a Patient Thinks about the Desert, poetry by Rick Anthony Furtak
Winter Solstice, poetry by Diana Howard
Blindfolds, Bruises, and Break-Ups, poetry by Jen Schneider
Songs of Snow and Silence, poetry by Jen Emery
INHABITANT, poetry by Charles Crittenden
Godless Grace, poetry by Michael Terence O'Brien
March of the Mindless, poetry by Thomas Walrod
In the Village That Is Not Burning Down, poetry by Travis Nathan Brown

about the author

Jesse Eagle lives and works in Colorado.